George Clare

The London Daily Stock and Share List

A course of lectures

George Clare

The London Daily Stock and Share List
A course of lectures

ISBN/EAN: 9783337428983

Printed in Europe, USA, Canada, Australia, Japan

Cover: Foto ©Andreas Hilbeck / pixelio.de

More available books at **www.hansebooks.com**

THE LONDON DAILY STOCK

AND

SHARE LIST:

A COURSE OF LECTURES

BY

GEORGE CLARE.

DELIVERED AT THE

Institute of Actuaries, Staple Inn Hall,

During the Session 1897-98.

LONDON:

CHARLES AND EDWIN LAYTON,

56, FARRINGDON STREET, E.C.

1898.

LECTURES

ON THE

LONDON DAILY STOCK AND SHARE LIST.

BY

Mr. GEORGE CLARE.

1897–1898.

INDEX.

I gladly respond to the invitation to introduce these Lectures on Finance with a few Prefatory words.

The more modern history of Life Assurance administration (especially in view of the continued decline in the rate of interest) has conclusively shown that, in addition to a sound mathematical equipment for discharge of his technical duties, the Actuary must be equally competent as a practical Financier. A theoretical acquaintance with financial problems and their relations, such as can be obtained from the study of books, is not simply futile but delusive also, and, indeed, dangerous, when confronted with the actual treatment of monetary affairs. As in all other departments of practical labour, capacity and judgment can alone be adequately cultivated by means of direct experience and examination of the course of financial movements, with their uniformities and interactions. The essential distinction between Theory and Practice is especially manifest in work like ours. In the interpretation of Nature, a Theory deduced and generalized from actual observations and experiments may be entertained by a student as useful and valuable information quite independent of experiments of his own; but, in Practical work, theoretical principles must absolutely be combined with direct experimental knowledge in one and the same person. The *passive* sense of vision, to adopt an illustration, affords but an imperfect and fragmentary acquaintance with the properties of phenomena: the *active* muscular sense must be exercised in order to secure that complex and co-ordinated knowledge which expresses the nature of the objects examined.

And, similarly with all masses of social facts dependent upon the operation of the human Will and motives, it will be discovered that commercial arrangements exhibit no arbitrary character but involve processes and results of causal and approximately calculable nature. On this ground, the empirical generalizations thus deduced enter within the range of general Science.

It is obvious that, in the early stage of an Actuarial Student's progress, this direct and intimate method of study is not feasible; and the sole efficient mode of training is to induct him into the consideration of such problems by means of Lectures which embody the experience and discriminated learning of *practical experts*. Hence the origin of these Lectures as an implement of Instruction in extension of the original design contemplated by the Founders of the Institute of Actuaries.

But the student must carefully observe that these Lectures do not constitute a sufficient Corpus in themselves of information or enquiry; they are to be accepted as providing *hints* for personal study and investigation: they are intended to assist in the stimulation and direction of the student's own observing and reflecting powers, and will prove idle and useless, as an *Educative* instrument, unless the individual mental activity is called simultaneously into play. The student must apply their teaching to the direct examination and consideration by himself of the course of the Money Market as presented in the newspapers; the dissection of the accounts and financial records of Companies; and the ascertainment and analysis of the influences and factors which affect the monetary values (as the expression of Demand and Supply) of pecuniary Interests.

In connection with the subject, it is very important to become early acquainted, for the purpose of avoiding wide-spread misconceptions, with the genuine scope and necessarily restricted nature of Political Economy; and I venture, accordingly, to suggest to the student two very brief but luminous references, which may be readily. grasped, and which will prove of helpful value in his enquiries,—namely, (i) "The Postulates of English Political Economy", by Bagehot (Students' Edition), pp. 7, 8, 9, 21, and 32; and (ii) Volume I of Buckle's "History of Civilization in England" (New Edition), p. 249, and Volume III, pp. 305–309, and 314.

I venture, further, as the "conclusion of the whole matter", to emphasize the proposition that, in the complete government of Life Assurance business, every administrative and financial element of its working is related intimately to *Actuarial* knowledge and aptitude. Omitting the methods of Valuation and Distribution, which are, by universal admission, of an exclusively Actuarial character, I would add that every question of expenses; the discussion of every Investment of every description; and the consideration of the modes of extending business, are not simply dependent, as is too frequently assumed, upon native or acquired acumen and commercial shrewdness and foresight, but, by reason of their *financial* aspects, are essentially connected with sound and sagacious Actuarial learning, and—distinctly bearing, as they accordingly do, upon systems of *Valuation* and *Distribution*— demand the skill of the trained Actuary for their fitting adjustment to these large and vital departments of his work. In brief, the successful administration of a Life Office, even regarded solely from the administrative and financial points of view, requires, as the controlling and supervising force, a competent Actuarial Education.

T. E. YOUNG.

14th June, 1898.

LONDON DAILY STOCK AND SHARE LIST.

FIRST LECTURE.

[Delivered 13 December 1897.]

GENTLEMEN, as you will see from the syllabus that has
been circulated, I have undertaken to deliver a short course of
lectures, with the object of introducing to you that somewhat
formidable-looking document, the London Daily Stock and
Share List, and also of making you acquainted, as far as time
will permit, with some portion of its contents. But as I have
not imposed this task upon myself with a view to converting
you into either "bulls" or "bears", I shall avoid discussing the
merits or the demerits of the securities enumerated in the List
in their character of investments or of speculations, but shall
confine myself to directing your attention to the nature and
to the distinctive peculiarities of the classes into which they
are grouped. I also purpose treating the subject historically,
as I am convinced that in all cases it is far easier to comprehend and co-ordinate the inherent qualities of a security
if we know something of its origin and of the early stages of
its development.

The Official List, I may begin by informing you, claims to
possess a very respectable antiquity. According to Lord
Macaulay, the business of stock-jobbing first assumed
importance a few years after the Revolution, from which
period we, as a matter of fact, date the beginnings of our
development into a nation of shopkeepers. Prior to the

Revolution there existed no stocks to deal in: which is a simple reason why the business was unknown. But about three years after the establishment of the Bank of England, the existence of a recognized market in securities was signalized by the appearance of a so-called "Course of Exchange", which came out twice a week, and which at the outset contained six securities only. This was in 1697, exactly 200 years ago, so that we may consider we are celebrating its bi-centenary here to-night. In 1797, a century later, the number of securities had grown to 20, but in 1897 it has increased to something like 3,000—and what is more, the number is being added to every month, at a rate which must bring despair to the soul of the publisher. What the List will be like in 1997, I dare not venture to prophecy, but it certainly looks as though long before then it will have to be published in sections. I may remark, in passing, that those who practised the business of stock-jobbing in early days, do not somehow appear to have gained the esteem of their contemporaries, for you will find if you refer to an original, or early, edition of Dr. Johnson's dictionary, that a stock-jobber is there defined (and this is not in jest, but in sober earnest) as "a low wretch, who gets money by buying and selling shares in the funds." Whether Dr. Johnson had ever been induced by by one of these "low wretches" to sell a "bear" of "shares in the funds", and got "cornered" over the operation, history does not tell us, but the definition is so spiteful that I "hae ma doots." To-day's List, then, contains the names and descriptions of upwards of 3,000 securities, practically the whole of which, with the exception of the first group "British Funds, &c.", have been called into existence since 1837. I know of no more striking proof of the enormous growth of our national wealth and resources during the 60 years of the Queen's reign. But without going back so far as that, let me take half the period. In the current volume of the Stock Exchange Official Intelligence, there is an article written by Sir Henry Burdett in which he points out the amazing fact that the total nominal value, so far as it can be ascertained, of the securities listed on the 1st of January 1867—only the other day, as it were—was £2,362,000,000, but that on the 1st of January 1897, the total nominal value was £6,065,000,000, so that in the last 30 years alone the British public have absorbed something like £4,000,000,000 of securities, and are still clamouring for more. At the present time our savings as a nation amount to about £200,000,000 a year—I should say considerably more rather than less, but that is a very safe estimate—and if we continue to grow rich at the same rate of progression, we shall require an outlet during the next 30 years for something like 6,000 to 8,000 million pounds of surplus capital. Well, I suppose some outlet will be found for it, as one always has been found, but on looking through the List, I must confess that I am quite unable to discover it. As to the first group, "British Funds, &c.", the National Debt is being fast paid off, while as regards municipalities and colonies, I think you will agree that they have already borrowed quite as much as appears justifiable. Foreign countries—the next head—have also had more of our money than is good either for them or for us. Our railway system, too, is practically complete; and so on throughout the list. Every channel, in fact, appears to be full to overflowing. It may be, however, that the development of electricity may in some way supply an opening, or it is also possible that a great war—*the* great war of the future—may swiftly sweep away the accumulations of a century of peace. Before concluding these prefatory remarks, it just occurs to me to say that if any of you wish to take up a congenial and original line of research— original, that is to say, as far as I know—I think I can suggest one. It would be very interesting, namely, to know the comparative yield during the last 30 years of each of the principal groups of securities. Suppose, for instance, a capitalist, on the 1st of January 1867, had invested a stated sum in Consols, would he have done better or worse to have spread his money over an assortment of English railway stocks? and in like manner, taking of course the dividends into account, what would the result have been if he had divided it amongst American Railway bonds or foreign stocks? You would, of course, have to allow for the losses caused by defaults and re-organizations, &c. I simply throw out the suggestion for what it may be worth;—the ground I am sure is fruitful, but whether the seed is worth growing is another matter. Turning now to the List we first notice that it is published by Mr. J. G. Wetenhall, and here I may remark, as a noteworthy circumstance, that the same name has been connected with the List for upwards of a century, at it is recorded in the archives of the Stock Exchange that in November 1787, Mr. E. Wetenhall was unanimously elected publisher by the members. That is followed by a notification that the List is published under the authority of the Committee of the Stock Exchange, and the superintendence of the Secretary of the Share and Loan department; but closely on the heels of this notification comes another that "the titles are taken from the securities as issued." I think there is more in this latter clause than meets the eye. You may take it for granted, I think, that although the List is under official supervision, yet the mere fact of a security being described in a certain manner is no guarantee whatever that it corresponds to such description. If, for instance, a stock or bond is described as "first mortgage", the buyer is not to assume without further enquiry, either that the mortgage actually is a first charge, or even that there exists any mortgage at all. The List, large as it is, does not claim to contain every share which is quoted on the Stock Exchange. Dealings take place every day in hundreds of shares which are not listed. Admission to the privilege of official quotation—for it is a privilege, and confers a certain status on an undertaking—depends to a certain extent (assuming that there exist no special grounds for exclusion) upon the importance of the concern, and this is gauged generally by its magnitude. Hence numbers of small companies have to be shut out, not because there is any question as to their *bonâ fides*, but simply because the inclusion of these small fry would render the List so bulky as to impair its utility. So far, however, as mining shares are concerned, there appears to exist some prejudice against them on the part of the Committee, as in no other way is it possible to explain the exclusion of so many well known concerns.

You will observe that the prices in the List are arranged in two columns, headed "Closing" and "Business done." Of these the "Closing quotations" are merely valuations and are not official in any sense whatever, which is a fact which I commend to your careful notice, because it is one as to which considerable misapprehension appears to prevail. The publisher of the List depends upon the dealers in the market to give him what they consider to be a fair estimate of the market value of the different stocks at the close of the day, but beyond the fact that the boards on which the clerk marks down the prices that have been supplied to him are hung up in the "House" for the inspection of members, no supervision whatever is exercised over these appraisements. In the case of securities that are currently dealt in, they afford, of course, a close and reliable indication of the value, but in regard to those in which transactions occur only rarely, the "Closing quotation" is frequently quite nominal and is only to be looked upon as an expert's opinion of the price at which business might perhaps be done. The closing quotation is useful, however, in one respect. If a broker on going into the market finds it impossible to deal at the quoted price, he can insist on having it altered to the limits at which he can deal. What is true of the closing quotation also applies to the well-known "tape" prices supplied by the Exchange Telegraph Company. These are likewise in no way official; but the dealer who supplies each particular price is held responsible for it, and if, when challenged by a broker, he refuses to deal, the quotation is not allowed to appear again. Under these circumstances you will easily understand that it is by no means a simple matter to assess the value of a parcel of stock, if required for probate or other purposes, and if this duty should ever devolve upon you, I can only advise you not to trust to the List quotation, but to call in the advice of a broker or other expert. The official part of the quotation is that which under the head "Business done" records the transactions that have actually taken place. When a broker concludes a bargain on the Stock Exchange, it is competent to him to have it "marked" if he so pleases. This is accomplished by passing a slip containing the necessary particulars to one of the clerks of the House, who officially registers the price by writing it on a certain board kept for that purpose, from whence it is copied down for publication in the List. The figures registered must be the actual market prices, and if any member considers the marking to be outside the current quotation, he may at once call the attention to it of two members of the Committee, who, if they find the objection justified, will order the marking to be expunged. By asking his broker to get a bargain marked, a buyer can, therefore, always satisfy himself that there has been no collusion between broker and jobber, and that the purchase or sale in which he is interested has been in all respects a genuine one. It is neither obligatory nor usual to give notice of every transaction. If a broker, for instance, buys at a lower or sells at a higher price than one already marked, he might not think it necessary to mark afresh. If Consols, for instance, are already marked 112¾, 113 on the board, business done at either of those rates, or at any fraction between them, would fall within the existing markings, so that "112¾, 113" may either mean two transactions at those respective prices or may represent 100 different transactions that have taken place within those limits. It should also be borne in mind that many bargains are not allowed to be marked, even if the broker should be anxious to do so. Up to the price of 30 no bargain may be marked at a smaller fraction than $\frac{1}{16}$, and at 30 or over, no bargain may be marked at a smaller fraction than $\frac{1}{8}$. Hence the thousands of bargains that are transacted at thirty-second prices are entirely excluded, and so are the majority of those at sixteenths. As to the amount of Stock in which business has been done the List affords us no information whatever, and a marking that represents a turnover of £20,000 may come to be sandwiched between two others that stand for less than a tithe of that amount. It is usual, however, to specially distinguish bargains in small bonds, or those in which an exceptional amount has changed hands at special prices. On the New York Stock Exchange, as some of you may have noticed, the number of shares dealt in is officially registered each day, and the magnitude of the daily turnover is an unerring guide to the activity of the market; but here in London, the only indication we possess to help us in that respect is the number of markings. If these are unusually numerous, we know that it has been a busy day in that particular market, but as to whether the dealings have amounted to 1,000 shares or 100,000 we are left quite in the dark. Business may be done either for "Money" or for the "Account"—that is to say, either for prompt settlement or for settlement on the next account day; but the great bulk of the transactions are for the "Account", and the quotation, unless otherwise stated, is to be so understood. There are two settlements per month, one towards the middle and one towards the end, but in Consols there is only one settling day, usually on or about the 3rd. All quotations, except those of Indian rupee paper, of some Indian railway debentures, and perhaps of one or two others, which are regarded as money market securities, include the interest that will have accrued on the security up to selling day. The seller makes the buyer a present of it, so to say. Suppose, for instance, that to-day I had bought £1,000 Argentine 1886 loan, which is quoted in the List at 93¼, 94¼, and on which the interest is due 1st January, I should have to pay for the stock on settling day—the day after to-morrow—but on the 1st January I receive interest, not from the 15th of December, but from the 1st of last July, so that actually the quotation includes $5\frac{1}{2}$ months' interest at 5 per-cent. To arrive at the real cost of the stock, therefore, I must deduct this accrued interest, and if I wish to be perfectly accurate in my book-keeping, I must take care on the 1st of January not to pass the whole coupon to revenue account, but to book only one-twelfth to income and the remaining eleven-twelfths to the credit of Argentine 1886 Loan, which stock will then stand in my ledger at its true net cost. As a consequence of this practice of including interest in the quotation, prices ought in theory to rise after each settlement (other things being equal) by about the amount of a fortnight's interest, and, when the dividend comes off, ought to undergo a fall of equal extent with its value. When 3 per-cent Local Loans Stock, for instance, is marked x. d. you will find that it falls $\frac{3}{4}$ per-cent, while Canadian Government 4 per-cent Guaranteed Bonds, on which the dividend is payable half-yearly, fall 2 per-cent when marked x. d., and so does the Turkish 1855 loan. In those exceptional cases—and they are very exceptional—in which interest is not included in the quotation, the buyer gives the seller, in addition to the market price, the interest accrued from the date of the last dividend-payment to the date on which he pays for the stock; and the quotation, so far as interest is concerned, need never vary. In one very important instance, however, which stands alone, this usage produces a somewhat remarkable effect. For Stock Exchange purposes the enfaced promissory notes of the Indian Government which are expressed as payable (both principal and interest) in rupees, and which go by the name of Rupee Paper, are quoted at so much per-cent in sterling, the rupee being calculated at the fixed conventional exchange of 2s. (that is to say, "Rupee Paper, 60" means £60 for 1,000 rupees) and the accrued interest, which has to be paid by the buyer, is also taken at the same rate of 2s. a rupee. Now the annual interest at $3\frac{1}{2}$ per-cent on 1,000 rupees is 35 rupees, equal to about 3 per month, so that if I buy £100 Rupee Paper a month after the interest was paid I shall have to give the seller, in addition to the price, three rupees, or 6s. for the accrued interest. But the rupee for which I am paying the seller 2s. is really only worth 1s. 3d., so that I lose 9d. per rupee, and that makes, you will find, about ⅛ per-cent per month. Consequently, so long as the Indian exchange stands at 1s. 3d., Rupee Paper will be worth ⅛ per-cent less for every month's interest that the buyer has to pay, and if it stood say at 61 the day the dividend came off, we should expect to see it a month afterwards at 60⅞; four months after at 60½, and so on. Instead, therefore, of the price remaining stationary, or of its rising from settlement to settlement, as is the case with other securities, and falling back again when the interest is paid, the price gradually declines (assuming the exchange to be steady at 1s. 3d., and other things being equal) at the rate of ⅛ per-cent per month, and the day it is marked x. d. goes up again to starting point. I must tax your patience a little longer upon this subject of accrued interest. In order to arrive at the actual cost of a stock purchase, it is necessary, as I said, to deduct from its price the interest that has been accumulating since the last dividend was received, and this is a fact we must carefully bear in mind whenever we have occasion to compare the yield of different investments. Thus, a 4 per-cent stock at 101, the dividends on which are due January and July, is not really so dear to-day as a 4 per-cent stock at par on which the dividends are due in June and December, because, of course, the price of the former includes 5 months' more interest, equal to 1⅔ per-cent, than that of the latter. Then, again, the question of interest must be carefully considered if you should have occasion to compare the foreign price of a security with the London price, or, what is much the same thing, if you should have to work out the cost of any stock from a foreign quotation; and as I have little doubt that insurance companies with huge funds to dispose of will sooner or later find it repay them to scrutinize the Continental Stock Exchange Lists in search of suitable investments, I hope you will not consider that I am wasting your time if I go into this matter rather more fully than might otherwise appear necessary. In the case of stocks quoted both in London and abroad a comparison of the respective prices constitutes what is called an "arbitrage" calculation, and the object of such calculations, when treated as a special business, is to take advantage of existing differences in value by buying in the cheapest and selling in the dearest market. Suppose, for instance, we know the price of a stock at A and the exchange between A and B, we can by a simple calculation ascertain the corresponding price of the stock at B. In like manner, if we knew the price at B and the rate of exchange, we can work out the price at A. This is called the " arbitrated " price or parity. Then, again, if we know the price at A and the price at B, we can, by a comparison of those prices, ascertain the rate of exchange between A and B, as established by these prices. This is called the " arbitrated par of exchange", and is arrived at, as you see, by buying the stock in one place and selling it in another. In actual practice the arbitrated par of exchange is very rarely considered, but in theory it plays an important part. As an example of calculations of arbitrated prices, let us take a simple case. If, for instance, Chartered shares are quoted at £3 in London, and the exchange between London and Paris is 25.25, what is the arbitrated price in Paris?

$$\text{Francs ?} = 1 \text{ Chartered share.}$$
$$1 = 3 \text{ £}$$
$$1 = 25.25 \text{ francs.}$$
$$\overline{}$$
$$75.75 \text{ francs.}$$

The arbitrated price is 75¾, and if the shares stand higher in Paris (allowing for all expenses of transmission) it will pay to buy them in London and sell them in Paris; if they are lower than 75¾, it will pay to buy them in Paris and sell them in London.

Or we may state the equation from the Paris point of view: that is to say, if Chartereds stand there at 75¾, and the cheque rate is 25.25, what is the arbitrated price in London ?

$$\text{£?} = 1 \text{ share.}$$
$$1 = 75.75 \text{ francs}$$
$$25.25 = 1 \text{ £}$$
$$\overline{}$$
$$3 \text{ £}$$

Here, again, if the London price is so much above £3 as to leave a profit after covering expenses, it will pay to buy in Paris and sell simultaneously in London ; or, if lower, to reverse the operation.

Lastly, suppose we have to remit to Paris, and it occurs to us to ask whether it would be cheaper to send Chartered shares than to buy a cheque. What exchange will Chartered shares give if we buy them here at £3 and sell them in Paris at 75¾ ?

$$\text{Francs ?} = £1.$$
$$£3 = 1 \text{ share.}$$
$$1 = 75.75 \text{ francs.}$$

$$25.25 \text{ francs.}$$

This is the arbitrated par of exchange as arrived at from a comparison of the respective prices of Chartered shares, but, as I have already said, an arbitrated par is valueless in practice, owing to the expenses that such an operation would entail.

So far as the theory of arbitrage goes, these three examples present the whole of it; but when we attempt to apply its principles to the prices of stocks quoted abroad *as well as in London*, we encounter at the outset a slight difficulty. The interest on the majority of such stocks is payable abroad, and whenever the interest on a stock is payable abroad the capital, you will find, is expressed in foreign currency.

Take an American railway bond, for instance; if the coupon is payable in London, the bond is expressed in sterling; if in London and New York, the bond is in both sterling and dollars; if in New York only, the bond is in dollars only. Again, the interest on Austrian silver rente is payable in Vienna, and the capital is in florins; on Dutch rente in Amsterdam, and the capital is in guilders; on French rente in Paris, and the capital is in francs; and so on.

But observe. If a bond or stock, the capital of which is expressed in a foreign currency, is dealt in or quoted in London, it is the custom of the Stock Exchange to buy and sell in sterling, and to convert the foreign money into pounds at a fixed conventional exchange, which, though not in each instance stated in the List (on page 2 a number of these stocks with " coupons payable abroad " are grouped together), is well known to all who have dealings in such securities. The Austrian florin, for instance, is taken at 2s., while the Dutch florin, which has about the same value, is only taken at 1s. 8d.; the franc is reckoned at 25 to the £; the mark at 1s. each; the American dollar at 4s. each, and so on.

A moment's consideration will convince you of the advantage of this plan, which is a custom of the Bourses all over the world. As things are, buyer and seller haggle over the price, and as soon as they arrive at an understanding on that point, the bargain can be concluded; but if the exchange were not fixed, they would have to haggle over the rate of exchange as well, and it would take just twice as long to do the business. Whether the fixed exchange is for or against the buyer does not really matter in the least, because any difference is taken into account in the price. But the fixed exchange is not the only difficulty we shall have to contend with. Another, and to the novice a more perplexing one, is that of interest. In London, as we have seen, the accrued interest is included in the price of the stock, and the same practice obtains in Paris and in New York. London, Paris, and New York quote net prices, but on almost all the foreign Bourses—Amsterdam, Berlin, Antwerp, Brussels, Copenhagen, St. Petersburg, Vienna, Hamburg, &c.,—the interest which has accrued on the stock since the payment of the last coupon is added to the price quoted in the List. This interest is always taken on the nominal amount of the stock, and is charged at the rate which the stock actually bears, but in the case of shares, with varying dividends, it is taken at a conventional rate (in Germany generally at 4 per-cent), which is usually stated in the foreign Lists side by side with the quotation. Now, let us see whether we can turn our information to any practical use.

I propose to take the prices of a few illustrative stocks from the foreign telegrams in to-day's *Times*, and to state the equations for you, but shall leave you to work out the parities for yourselves, and to compare them with the actual London prices in the List.

FRENCH 3½ PER-CENT RENTE. PARIS PRICE, 106¾.

The interest on this stock is payable abroad, and the capital is expressed in francs, which are taken here at 25 to the £. The actual exchange for cheques on Paris is 25.18½.

$$£? = 100 £ \text{ stock},$$
If £ stock $1 = 25$ francs stock,
if francs stock $100 = 106.75$ francs,
and francs $25.185 = 1 £.$

CHESAPEAKE AND OHIO 4½ PER-CENT BONDS.
NEW YORK PRICE, 81.

Interest payable New York. Capital expressed in dollars.
Fixed exchange, $5 = £1. Actual exchange $4.86 = £1.

$$£ ? = 100 £ \text{ stock.}$$
$$\text{If } £ \text{ stock } 1 = 5 \$ \text{ stock.}$$
$$\text{If } \$ \text{ stock } 100 = 81 \$$$
$$\text{If } \$ \qquad 4.86 = 1 £.$$

PRUSSIAN 3 PER-CENT CONSOLS. BERLIN PRICE, 97.40.

Interest payable Berlin on 1 April and 1 October (not
included in the price). Capital expressed in Reichsmarks.
Fixed exchange m. 20 = £1. Actual exchange, 20.37½.

N.B.—In Germany and on the Continent generally, the
year is taken in interest calculations at 360 days, and the
month at 30 days.

$$£ ? = 100 £ \text{ stock.}$$
$$\text{If } £ \text{ stock } 1 = 20 \text{ m. stock.}$$
$$\text{If m. stock } 100 = *98.02½ \text{ m.}$$
$$\text{If m. } \qquad 20.37½ = 1 £.$$

* 98.02½ is the price (97.40), plus 2½ months' accrued interest (1 October to
15 December), at 3 per-cent.

MEXICAN 6 PER-CENT 1888 LOAN. BERLIN PRICE, 96.60.

Interest payable quarterly in London. Capital expressed
in sterling. Fixed exchange in Berlin, £1 = m. 20. Actual
exchange, 20.37½.

$$£ ? = 100 £ \text{ stock.}$$
$$\text{If } £ \text{ stock } 1 = 20 \text{ m. stock.}$$
$$\text{If m. stock } 100 = *97.85 \text{ m.}$$
$$\text{If m. } \qquad 20.37½ = 1 £.$$

* 97.85 is the price (96.60), plus 2½ months' accrued interest (1 October to
15 December) at 6 per-cent.

ITALIAN 5 PER-CENT RENTE. BERLIN PRICE, 95.10.

Interest payable Paris on 1 January and 1 July, less 20
per-cent Italian tax. Capital expressed in francs. Fixed

exchange in Berlin fcs. 100 = m. 80 ; Fixed exchange in London, fcs. 25 = £1. Actual exchange, Berlin on London, 20.37½.

$$£ \; ? = 100 \; £ \text{ stock.}$$

If £ stock   1 =   25 francs stock.
If francs stock 100 =   80 m. stock.
If m. stock   100 = *96.88 m.
If m.   20.37½ =   1 £.

* 96.88 is the price (95.10), plus 5½ months' accrued interest (1 July to 15 December), at 4 per-cent.

AUSTRIAN SILVER RENTE.   VIENNA PRICE, 101½.

Interest payable Vienna, less 16 per-cent tax.   Capital expressed in florins.   Fixed exchange, fl. 10 = £1.   Actual exchange, 12.07.

$$£ \; ? = 100 \; £ \text{ stock.}$$

If £ stock   1 =   10 florins stock.
If fl. stock 100 = *103.42 florins.
If fl.   12.07 =   1 £.

* 103.42 is the price (101.50), plus 5½ months' accrued interest (1 July to 15 December), 4½ per-cent.

In the case of stocks not quoted in London, and in which the question of the fixed exchange does not arise, the foreign price, plus interest, if divided by the sight-exchange, gives the cost in London, to which must be added the expense of getting the stock over.

Those of you who may have studied the subject of the foreign Exchanges will probably remember to have read that a rising rate is frequently held in check, and prevented from reaching gold point by arbitrage operations in stocks, and you will now be better able to understand what that statement means. The point is this : the higher the exchange rises, the less it costs to remit from this side, and the less the remittance costs, the cheaper the stock works out.

Thus, if Chartered shares stand at £3 in London, and at 75.30 in Paris, when the exchange is at 25.10, the price would be the same on both sides ; but if the exchange rose to 25.22½, the parity would work out ½ per-cent cheaper, and it might then pay to buy the shares in Paris, and sell them in London. If such operations were carried out on a large scale, it is easily seen that the increased supply of London paper in Paris (or the increased demand for Paris paper in London) would stay the further rise in the exchange until the price of the shares adjusted themselves to the changed conditions of supply and demand by rising a fraction in Paris and falling a fraction in London.

LONDON DAILY STOCK AND SHARE LIST.

SECOND LECTURE.

[Delivered 10 January 1898.]

AT our last session we discussed the history and composition of the Official List, and we now proceed to examine its contents. It starts well, you will see, for in the first group we have the pick of the basket. It begins by setting out those securities which constitute an *absolute first charge* on the wealth and industry of the richest kingdom of the world, and of its greatest dependency. Under the superscription of British Funds, &c., we find all the Parliamentary Stocks and Government Securities of the United Kingdom: all those securities, the interest on which is guaranteed by Parliament, the stocks of the Bank of England and Ireland, and those forming the debt of India; the all-round high quality of this little assortment being attested by the fact that it is lawful for a trustee, unless expressly forbidden by the instrument creating the trust, to invest any trust funds in his hands in every one of them, except Rupee Paper. The leading items in the group are, of course, those which make up the National Debt, and this it will be well to consider as a whole, before we proceed to examine its separate parts.

Our National Debt, like that of most other Great Powers, is in the main a war debt; but though it was in the reign of William the Third that the practice of borrowing money to carry on war was first introduced together with its corollary, the Funding system, it would be a mistake to imagine that the device of meeting the exigencies of the State by loans was imported into our Island by William's Dutch advisers. The expedient of anticipating revenue by borrowing at short date was of great antiquity, and in times when the system of tax collection was far less prompt than it is now was unavoidable. It is one, moreover, that prevails in a familiar shape to this day, for in every quarter when there is a deficiency in the means to meet the charges upon the Consolidated Fund, advances to the required amount are obtained from the Bank of England (or the Bank of Ireland), which are paid off from the accruing revenue of the ensuing quarter and which constitute, therefore, a loan in anticipation of revenue. In the Exchequer and Audit Department Act of 1866, you find it enacted that "At the close of each of the "quarters ending on the 31st day of March, the 30th day of "June, the 30th day of September, and the 31st day of "December in every year, the Treasury shall prepare an "account of the income and charge of the Consolidated Fund "in Great Britain and in Ireland for such quarter, and the "charges for the Public Debt, due on the 5th day of April, "the 5th day of July, the 10th day of October, and the 5th "day of January, shall be included in the accounts of the said "charge for the quarters ending on the days preceding the "latter dates; and a copy of such account shall forthwith be "transmitted by the Treasury to the Comptroller and Auditor- "General; and if it shall appear by such account that the "income of the Consolidated Fund in Great Britain or in "Ireland for the quarter is not sufficient to defray the charge "upon it, the Comptroller and Auditor-General, if satisfied of "the correctness of the deficiency, shall certify the amount "thereof to the Bank of England or to the Bank of Ireland, "as the case may be, and upon such certificates the said Banks "shall be authorized to make advances from time to time "during the succeeding quarter, on the application of the "Treasury, by writing in a form to be from time to time "determined by them to an amount not exceeding in the "aggregate the sums specified in such certificates; and all "such advances shall be placed to the credit of the Exchequer "Acounts at the said Banks and be available to satisfy the "Orders for Credits granted, or to be granted, upon the said "accounts by the Comptroller and Auditor-General; and the

" principal and interest of all such advances shall be paid out " of the growing produce of the Consolidated Fund in the " said succeeding quarter." The Government cannot borrow without express permission, and the Act was passed to give them that permission. What really dates from the Revolution, as Macaulay points out, is not the system of borrowing but the system of funding. Merely to contract debts was no novelty, but the system introduced by William the Third, of honestly paying them, was a genuine innovation. The origin of our indebtedness as a nation may be traced to a piece of chicanery on the part of Charles the Second. After the Restoration, the London goldsmiths, who were bankers as well as dealers in the precious metals, lent the Government about £1,300,000, which had been deposited with them by their customers. This money the King appropiated to himself in 1672 by suddenly shutting up the Exchequer, and informing the lenders that, though it was not convenient to let them have the principal, he should be pleased to go on paying them interest. Many years afterwards, in 1701, the half of this sum was formally acknowledged by Parliament as a national obligation, so that in point of origin it forms the oldest part of the public debt. During the war waged by King William against the French allies of his father-in-law, it was found impracticable to meet the excessive expenditure by revenue raised within the year, and recourse was therefore had to loans. At first the Government felt its way cautiously; it borrowed only for short periods, promised to repay by instalments, and pledged particular taxes to secure the return of the principal and interest. These taxes were to be levied only for a limited number of years, and it was expected that their produce would discharge the debt within the period for which they were granted. In 1692, for instance, a law was passed imposing certain new duties on beer and other liquors, and it was ordered that these duties should be kept in the exchequer separate from all other receipts, and that they should form a *fund*, on the credit of which a million was to be raised by life annuities. Had the war quickly terminated, this and similar arrangements would probably have been adhered to; but its long duration, and the new emergencies to which it gave rise, rendered it necessary to put the redemption off to a future day. The loans had to be renewed, and the taxes continued; the pretence of repayment was gradually abandoned; and the country was at last committed to the plan of paying interest only, and of allowing the principal to stand over as a permanent liability. Once fairly entered upon, this system of permanent borrowing went steadily on from year to year, and under one administration after another, until, at the termination of the long struggle which ended in 1815, the debt, funded and unfunded, reached its highest point of nine hundred millions (in this sum I include the value of the terminable annuities which at that time were not reckoned part of the debt), having thus attained its maximum in the short space of about a century and a quarter. Whether those who incurred that liability had the right to cast so large a share of its burden upon posterity is a question to which there are two sides. The annual charge for interest and sinking fund is so large an item of our national expenditure, that its extinction would create a revolution in our finances, and it would be very agreeable, no doubt, if we could awake one morning to find ourselves free of the six hundred millions of debt contracted by Mr. Pitt and his successors—it would be very agreeable, that is to say, if we could be rid of it without otherwise altering our circumstances. But would our circumstances be the same? Is it not likely, as the late Lord Iddesleigh, who gave considerable attention to the subject, appears to have thought, that if that money had been raised by excessive taxation, the load would have been too great for the springs of industry and commerce to bear, and hence that our national resources at the present time would be far more seriously crippled than they actually are by the burden of the debt? After all, it may possibly be better for us that Mr. Pitt allowed the money to fructify in the hands of our great-grandfathers, instead of forcing it out of their possession by taxation. It is generally admitted too, as an abstract principle, that the money cost of a struggle for national existence may, with justice and propriety, be left for succeeding generations to liquidate. The cost in blood and tears must be borne at the time, but the mere debit balance in the national ledger may be left for settlement in the future. I speak now, of course, of those great wars in which a nation fights for its life and liberty. As to the little wars which every generation has to engage in, which confer only a temporary benefit, and which are essentially the evils of a day, their cost, it is clear, is a charge against revenue and not against capital, and the Government that undertakes them, and which gains in popularity thereby, ought undoubtedly to settle the bill.

The public debt is of two descriptions. In addition to that greater portion which has solidified into a permanent shape, and which is known as the funded debt, there always exists a varying amount of indebtedness of a less degree of fixity known as the unfunded or floating debt. This consists of loans raised for short periods and for temporary purposes. It represents money borrowed from time to time to meet national expenses for which no provision has been made, or for which the provision made has either proved insufficient or not forthcoming at the time when wanted. Our credit as a nation, it is to be observed, is committed to the due payment of interest on both classes of obligation alike; but while on the former the State contracts to pay interest only, it undertakes, in regard to the latter, to discharge the principal as well as the interest. In other words, the State promises to pay off the unfunded debt on certain specified dates, but the funded debt it need never pay at all. The securities representing unfunded debt are, or rather were until recently, of three denominations, namely, Exchequer Bills, Exchequer Bonds, and Treasury Bills. For the invention of the Exchequer Bill we are indebted to the fertile genius of Charles Montague, William the Third's renowned Chancellor of the Exchequer. During the great re-coinage undertaken in that reign, the withdrawal of the old money appears to have proceeded more rapidly than the issue of the new, and the country fell into great distress for want of the currency needed to conduct its business. In order to fill the void, a clause was inserted at Montague's instance in the Ways and Means Bill of 1696, empowering the issue of interest-bearing Government paper, based on the security of the revenue, and in July of that year the first Exchequer Bills appeared. The success of the issue was great, and though intended merely as a temporary substitute for the new money then in course of manufacture, the country took to the Bills so kindly, even after the immediate necessity had passed away, that the Government decided on their permanent adoption, and they continued in use down to the present year. A newly-issued Bill bore interest coupons running for five years, but as the holder might claim repayment of the principal on any anniversary of the date of the Bill, it was practically twelve months' paper. To ensure convertibility, they were made receivable in payment of customs, excise, or other duties, at any time in the last six months of every year from the date of the Bill, and the interest due on them at the time of presentation was allowed in the payment. They were issued at two periods only, March and June, and the interest, which might not exceed 5½ per cent., was fixed half-yearly, and always at such a rate so as to keep the Bill at a slight premium. There was a very good reason for this practice. In case of an emergency, the Chancellor of the Exchequer might have had need to raise a few millions as quickly as possible, and by keeping the Exchequer Bill at a trifling premium, he could always be sure that a new issue at par would be eagerly taken up. Until the introduction of the Treasury Bill, the theory held with regard to the Exchequer Bill was that it provided a security of which not only was the repayment at par assured, but which, by bearing a variable interest, adjustable to the circumstances of the money market, should always preserve a fixed value, and hence be a suitable investment for floating money. In practice, however, the theory was never fully carried out, because the interest, instead of being adjusted from week to week, or even from month to month—as it would require to have been if the value of the principal was never to vary—was fixed for half a year in advance, during which period there was always the possibility, owing to unforeseen changes in the money market, of the Bill falling to a discount, as it frequently did. But apart from this drawback, the Exchequer Bill, it had long been evident, had had its day. It belonged to a time when the rate of interest on short loans did not fluctuate so often as it does now, and when the system of holding vast sums of money ready for short investment was unknown. The expedient, too, of permitting them to be used in payment of duties grew antiquated, and did not accord with modern ideas. Gradually the issue grew smaller, and finally, in 1897, it dwindled away altogether. In his Budget speech in April last, the Chancellor of the Exchequer, referring to this subject, said : " The unfunded debt, besides being reduced, has been " greatly simplified. It now consists solely of Treasury Bills. " The remnant of Exchequer Bonds borrowed by the First " Lord of the Admiralty to pay off the holders of consols, has " been paid off during the past year. Exchequer Bills have " ceased. That security which was invented 200 years ago

" by one of the greatest of my predecessors, Mr. Charles
" Montague, in order to effect a great re-coinage for the
" benefit of the country, has often stood the Treasury in good
" stead, and never more so than during the great war early in
" this century. But these Bills, issued as they were for terms
" of five years, the interest on them being fixed half-yearly
" by the Treasury, have become inconvenient. Certainly it
" was an invidious task to fix the interest on Exchequer Bills.
" You might fix it too high, and if you did, there was a loss
" to the Exchequer; if you fixed it too low, the holders of the
" Bills had a right to present them at certain periods in
" payment of duty. And in these days Treasury Bills issued
" for periods of not more than 12 months at a rate fixed by
" the competition of the market, are far more convenient, and
" a better form of security." The Exchequer Bond to which
the Chancellor of the Exchequer refers, was another form of
security invented by Mr. Gladstone in 1853. Bonds to bearer
are of course common enough now, but at that time they were
little known. The interest on the Exchequer Bond was to be
payable by coupon, and Mr. Gladstone thought that foreign
buyers of our investments would be likely to give the
preference to one of which the actual security itself would be
in their possession, and of which they could encash the interest
in whatever part of the world they might be by simply cutting
off and selling a coupon. For some reason or another the
Exchequer Bond was not a success, and for many years the public
heard no more of them, the few that came out at intervals
being issued to the National Debt Commissioners against
advances made out of the funds under their control. In 1889,
however, Mr. Goschen decided to resuscitate them, and a new
form of bond was prepared to meet modern requirements, but
these also were paid off last year, and now it is very likely
that we have seen the last of them. The third and last
division of the unfunded debt, and now in fact the only one,
is that of Treasury Bills. These are Money Market securities,
and, as they are not dealt in on the Stock Exchange, you will
not find them in the Official List; but that need not prevent us
from bestowing a little attention on them. I think I am
right in saying that the first conception of the Treasury
Bill is contained in a suggestion put forward by the late
Mr. Walter Bagehot, who, in an article in the *Economist* of 1876,
asked the very apposite question, " Why not issue Exchequer

Bills at short dates"? Up to that time, whenever it was the duty of the Chancellor of the Exchequer to raise money for temporary purposes, he had to choose between the Exchequer Bond and the 12 months' Exchequer Bill. On the former he could never hope to borrow at much less than 3 per-cent, and on the latter, although backed up by the finest credit in the world, the Government had just announced the rate to be 2 per-cent, while a private individual could, on the same day, have taken a three months' Bank Bill into the market and have borrowed on it at just half that rate. The fault, said Mr. Bagehot, lies in the present form of Exchequer Bill. It runs too long, and it is too clumsy. If the Government wish to take advantage of the tempting cheapness of the money available for this class of investment, let them issue a more handy and more negotiable security. For a three months' bill the market would be found willing to pay the best price, and the Government ought to study its wants. The wisdom of the advice was recognized in the proper quarter, and early in the following year the Chancellor of the Exchequer, Sir Stafford Northcote, introduced a Bill providing for the issue of a new form of floating debt obligation, to be known as a Treasury Bill. The Act imposed no restrictions on the Treasury in respect of the rate which it might pay— the rate on Exchequer Bills was limited to 5½ per-cent—but the term of the Bill was not to exceed 12 months. Immediately afterwards, in March 1877, tenders were invited for the first emission under the new plan, and to the gratification of those concerned, the Government succeeded in obtaining the best market rate. Being new and strange, however, the Treasury Bills were for some time looked upon rather shyly, but during the City of Glasgow Bank crisis, which occurred in 1878, French bankers manifested so strong a predilection for such perfectly A 1 paper as to give them the character of an international Bill, and from that time they have taken their proper place as the highest class of paper known to the market. From the point of view of the Chancellor of the Exchequer, Treasury Bills possess another excellent quality in addition to that of enabling him to borrow cheaply; they also enable him to spread the liabililty over the whole year. There was no legal reason why an Exchequer Bill should not bear date on any date that the Treasury might appoint, but the peculiarity of the interest conditions appeared to render it convenient to issue only twice a year, so that the danger of having to take them up was concentrated on two days only, whereas the three months' Treasury Bills are arranged in such a manner as to fall due about twice a month all the year round, and, at the worst, the Government could only have a small proportion thrown on its hands at one time. As the Treasury Bill bears no interest, the buyer pays the amount, less discount. In tendering for them, " the tenders must specify the net amount per-cent which will be given "; that is to say, instead of offering to take a 12 months' bill at 2½ per-cent, you bid £97. 10s. per-cent for it. Perhaps I need hardly mention that, as this is bankers' discount, and not true discount, the buyer at that price really obtains rather more than 2½ per-cent on his money.

Let us revert now for a moment to the loan that I spoke of as being raised in 1692. Its repayment, I told you, was secured by the hypothecation of certain fresh duties which were simultaneously imposed to an amount sufficient both to meet the interest and to redeem the principal by instalments. The borrowing system, of course, was then in its infancy, and the national credit consisted of little else than good intentions. The Stuarts had just been driven from the country, and the Government of William was far from firmly established. It was very natural, under these circumstances, that provision for paying back the money borrowed should be deemed an essential part of the scheme. To have attempted, indeed, to borrow, with the avowed intention of never repaying, would only have excited ridicule. Duties or taxes so assigned and set apart, as in this instance, were said to form a *fund*, and his claim upon some such specified *fund* constituted the lender's security.

This practice of the hypothecation of a specific branch of the revenue is a very common practice in the case of countries of inferior credit. The law authorizing the Argentine 1886 Loan, for instance, contains the following clause—" The " service of the loan shall be provided by the general " revenues of the country, the Custom House receipts remain- " ing specially appropriated to the necessary extent for the " annual service." A first-class State, such as England, Germany, France, Holland, &c., borrows, of course, upon its general credit; only a State which cannot do this proposes to mortgage a particular revenue. Security of that kind, even at its best, is very superficial, for if the country which mortgages its customs finds it impossible, or says it finds it impossible to pay, where is the imagined security? In order to realize it, the bondholder would have to usurp the government of the country, which is out of the question. Duties and taxes so assigned and set apart were described, I repeat, as a *fund,* and his *claim* upon some such specified fund constituted the lender's security. Gradually, however, by that process of contraction, which is the offspring of frequent repetition, dealing in *claims* on the funds, came to be spoken of as dealings in "the funds" simply, until, in course of time, the word "funds" almost lost its original signification of the security on which the loans were based, and acquired the new meaning, which it still retains, of the principal of the loans themselves. The use of "funds" in the sense of public debt is, therefore, a survival of the primitive practice. At the outset, again, funding a loan meant, as we have just seen, the provision of resources to extinguish the capital as well as cover the interest, and when the Government first began to contract permanent loans, and to charge the fund with the payment of interest only, this latter process was distinguished as *perpetual* funding; but the "perpetual" appears to have soon dropped away, and we are left with plain "funding" in the altered sense of appropriating revenue for the perpetual payment of interest alone. What we now mean when we speak of our "funded" debt is permanent debt, of which the interest is a perpetual charge on the Consolidated Fund. In modern times the meaning has undergone even further modification, for whereas the word originally indicated that the service of the loan was secured by a fund, and then that the service was secured, and the loan permanent or of long duration, we now either take the security for granted or treat it as a separate matter, and a so-called "funding operation," in many cases, signifies little more than the conversion of an immediate or a short-term debt into a long term or a perpetual debt.

The primitive practice of keeping a separate account of each loan, and of the taxes levied for its service, lasted only a few years. Some of the taxes left a deficit, while others produced a surplus; and the multiplicity of funds complicated the book-keeping. It was therefore decided, about 1715, to collect the various branches of revenue into three large groups, known as the General, the Aggregate, and the South Sea Funds, each of which was charged with the payment of certain specific annuities. This arrangement, though still involving a separate calculation at the Custom House for each of the different subsidies, was a distinct improvement over the former system, and for some time worked well enough; but long before the end of the century the country had outgrown it, and further simplification was urgently called for. In 1787, accordingly, Mr. Pitt pointed out to the fundholders that, as the credit of the country was committed to the fulfilment of all its obligations alike, the comparative priority of the various loans was more imaginary than real; and, on obtaining their consent to an amalgamation of the security, he abolished a distinction that had become practically valueless and established one single fund, to which he carried the whole of the permanent revenue, and to which he gave the name of "The Consolidated Fund." The principal and interest of the Unfunded Debt, and the whole of the perpetual annuities payable in respect of the Funded Debt, form a first charge upon and are payable out of this Consolidated Fund of the United Kingdom, without distinction or priority.

That greater portion of our national indebtedness, which is repayable only at the option of the Government, and not at the option of the annuitant, is called the Funded Debt, and is composed of the following stocks: Two-and-a-Half per-cent Annuities; Two-and-Three-quarters per-cent Annuities; and Two-and-Three-quarters per-cent Consolidated Stock, as well as the book-debts owing to the Banks of England and Ireland. To discover its first beginnings, we must look to the negotiations that led to the incorporation of the Bank of England. There can be little doubt that the Government then contemplated the contraction, for the first time, of a permanent debt; for though the Charter was made terminable in 1706, it is not to be supposed that the Government had any intention of withdrawing it after twelve years, or the Bank of asking for repayment. The advance by the Bank to the public of £1,200,000 in 1694 was therefore the foundation stone of our Funded Debt; and Bank of England Stock is the patriarch of the official List. The stock that takes the lead in our schedule—Two-and-a-Half per-cents—owes its origin, indirectly, to the discoveries of gold, between 1848 and 1851, in

California and Australia. As a consequence of those discoveries, which occasioned a great influx of the metal to this
country, the belief was strongly entertained 45 years ago, that
we were on the eve of a great and permanent reduction in the
value of money. In February, 1853, the rate of interest on
Exchequer Bills was cut down from 1½d. to 1d. per day, but
not one Bill was sent in for repayment, and they still stood at
a premium; and Consols were quoted at par. Rumours of a
projected reduction of interest on the Debt got abroad, and,
as the nation appeared to have fully prepared itself for a
conversion, Mr. Gladstone decided not to disappoint it. His
scheme, which was produced in March, had a two-fold object.
His minor aim, in which he succeeded, was to sweep away a
few remnants of old stocks connected with the South Sea
Company, that still encumbered the List; but his great purpose
was to lay the foundation of the stock of the future—of a
permanent form of irredeemable public debt (irredeemable,
that is to say, at the option of the holder), bearing interest at
2½ per-cent. To this end he offered to give, in exchange
for each £100 of Three per-cent Stock, yielding 60s. per-cent,
either £110 of Two-and-a-Half per-cent Stock, yielding
55s. per-cent, or £82½ of Three-and-a-Half per-cent Stock,
yielding a rather better income, namely, 57s. 9d. per-cent. In
both cases he guaranteed the holder against further interference
until 1894. The latter stock (the Three-and-a-Half per-cent.)
was created with a view to the convenience of those who might
prefer a larger present payment at the sacrifice of part of
their future capital, but as less than a quarter of a million was
applied for, it would seem that very few such people existed.
At any rate, the stock was a dead failure, and in 1894 it was
paid off and abolished. As to the Two-and-a-Half per-cents,
Mr. Gladstone's stock of the future, the only fault Parliament
could find with it was that it was a great deal too cheap, and
everyone confidently predicted that it would be taken with
avidity. The Opposition even professed great alarm at the
enormous increase of fifty millions in the capital of the debt
which would ensue if the holders of the existing five hundred
millions of Consols and Reduced Threes assented in a body, as the
City said they would, and to appease their fears, Mr. Gladstone
promised to allot only thirty millions to begin with, and to
extinguish the increase of capital by applying the annual
saving of ¼ per-cent interest to a sinking fund. To cut the

story short, the end of this much-belauded plan was that only *three millions* of the new stock were applied for. Before it could be fairly launched on the market, the political horizon had begun to cloud over and the coming event of the Russian war was casting its first shadow over the minds of far-seeing statesmen and capitalists. The year that had opened so auspiciously with bank rate at 2 per-cent and Consols at par, closed with money at 5 per-cent and Consols at 92½, and amid the general depression, the great conversion scheme of 1853 —the only prominent financial failure with which Mr. Gladstone's name is connected—suffered complete shipwreck. Over a quarter of a century was to pass away before a new generation of business men were to see Consols once more at par. It was not until November, 1880, that they again crept up to three figures, and that investors again began to ask themselves how soon the Government would feel itself bound, as guardian of the public purse, to make a fresh attempt at the inevitable reduction. If the credit of the country was now such as to enable it to borrow at less than 3 per-cent, it was, of course, incumbent on the Chancellor of the Exchequer to reconsider the terms of the bargain between the national debtor and the national creditor, and if possible to ease the burden of the taxes by inducing the fund-holder to accept a little less, or, if he proved obdurate, by borrowing elsewhere on lower terms and gradually paying him off; but it was not until 1884 that Mr. Childers made the anticipated proposal. This consisted of an offer to the holders of the Three-per-cents to exchange each £100 of stock yielding 60s. per-cent, into either £108 of Two-and-a-Half per-cent stock yielding 54s. per-cent, or £102 of a new Two-and-Three-quarters per-cent stock yielding 56s. 1d. per-cent. In this case, both stocks were made irredeemable until 1905, and, as in the case of Mr. Gladstone's conversion of 1853, the increase of capital in the case of the Two-and-a-Half per-cent Stock to be paid off by a sinking fund. The Two-and-a-Half per-cent Stock was Mr. Gladstone's old creation, which had mean-while been increased by sundry operations to fourteen millions, but Mr. Childers extended the period during which it was irre-deemable from 1894 to 1905. That the terms were very liberal was agreed on all hands, and it was generally expected that the response to the invitation would be practically unanimous. The general expectation, however, was again falsified; for the

c

option was only taken advantage of to the extent of nineteen-and-a-quarter millions of the old Two-and-a-Half per-cents, nearly thirteen millions of which were applied for by Government departments, and four-and-a-half millions of the new Two-and-Three-quarter per-cents, so that another small stock was thus added to the List. Politics could not be blamed this time for the want of success, yet there was evidently a miscalculation somewhere. The mistake, it would appear, was that of offering alternative stocks, instead of proposing a general and progressive reduction of interest in the existing stock. Like the proverbial bundles of hay, the two alternatives only served to render the investor undecided, and in the end to prevent him from accepting either, besides which, they also produced the more serious effect of causing the bankers to hold back. Why the latter should have refrained, as a body, from supporting the scheme was perfectly clear; they disliked seeing a great stock, such as consols was, split into halves, and, moreover, if they were to be forced into conversion, they at least wished to make sure, before committing themselves, which of the alternative stocks would command the wider market. They wanted, as Mr. Pickwick once advised, to shout with the largest crowd, and immediately it became evident that the fund-holders generally meant to hold on as long as possible to their beloved Three per-cents, all hope of a voluntary surrender on the part of the banks was at an end. The net result of the two conversions that we have been discussing, was the addition to the List of two new stocks, one of which is so small in amount that any inference drawn from a comparison between its price movements and those of Consols would hardly be reliable, but the other—the Two-and-a-Half per-cents—has on two occasions, when Consols were over par, served a most useful purpose. It has acted as a gauge, or testing machine, by which to ascertain the true value of the public credit, and, as the point is interesting, we will step aside for a moment to examine it. Consols, as we have seen, touched par in November 1880, but to save the trouble of deducting accrued dividend, we will compare the prices of the 6th January 1881, which are free of interest. The quotations were : 82 for the Two-and-a-Half per-cents, and 98¾ for Consols. Now, if a Two-and-a-Half per-cent stock is worth 82, a Three per-cent stock, which is based on precisely the same security, and the price of which is governed by the same considerations, ought to be worth one-fifth more, or 98⅖, but as Consols were in rather better demand at the time than the Two-and-a-Half per-cents, they were quoted a little higher, at 98¾, which, however, is quite near enough. Three years afterwards, in January 1884, on looking again at the price of the Two-and-a-Half per-cents, we find it has improved to 90⅜, and we naturally expect that the same flowing tide will have carried Consols up in a like proportion to 108¼. But, as a matter of fact, Consols only stood at 101¼; the reason of the check being that, as they were redeemable at par at any time after twelve months' notice, the buyer ran the risk of soon losing whatever premium he paid, and consequently felt it unsafe to go more than a point or two beyond par. We begin now to see the advantage of a reference to the Two-and-a-Half per-cents quotation. If Consols had been the only stock to go by, it would have been reasonable to infer from the current price that a Perpetual Government Annuity of £3 was worth no more than £101¼, whereas the real value, as made manifest by the price of the Two-and-a-Half per-cents, was over £108. For the time being, in fact, the price of the latter alone correctly gauged the actual value of the national credit, and deductions drawn from the price of consols were fallacious. In the speech introducing the conversion scheme of 1888, Mr. Goschen also took occasion to point out that while the Two-and-a-Half per-cents, which enjoyed an immunity from conversion for many years, were then quoted at 96, Consols, with this imminent danger hanging over them, were no higher than 102, and that under the circumstances the former were the genuine indicators of the real value of Government security.

We now come to Consols, "the historical stock of this country—the champion stock of the world", as Mr. Goschen enthusiastically termed it. There appears to exist a popular notion that Consols is a sort of generic name for all the Government stocks forming the Funded Debt, and that the separate headings in the schedule only serve to distinguish between the different species; but, strictly speaking, the term only applies, of course, to Consols proper, which is a stock that was formed in 1752, by *consolidating* into one, or, as we should now call it, unifying, a number of small stocks, all bearing 3 per-cent interest. The unified stock was entitled " Three per-cent Consolidated Annuities ", from which to plain

" Consols " was an easy transition. Other consolidated annuities, of higher denominations, afterwards appeared in the schedule, but the Three per-cents always retained their distinctive designation of " Consols ", both because they came first in point of time, and because they took the lead in the matter of magnitude. Owing to a change made in the system of funding about the year 1781, this particular stock was one that grew rapidly. Before that year the sound principle had been adhered to of varying the amount of the annuity according to circumstances, but of never selling it below par ; but in 1781, as the difficulty of raising money increased, the practice grew up of keeping the annuity invariable, and selling it for what it would fetch. The difference was this—under the old system, if it was required to raise £100 when the rate was 6 per-cent, the Government would have sold £100 6 per-cent stock at par. Under the new system it sold £200 3 per-cent stock at 50. Upon the capital of the Debt the consequences were deplorable. From the beginning of the American War to the end of the French War we borrowed 417 millions in money, but created 589 millions in stock, thus increasing the debt by 172 millions more than was necessary. In defence of this practice, it was maintained that the issue of loans at par at a time when the value of the national credit rose with every victory, and declined with every reverse, would have meant a sub-division of the debt into stock at all sorts of awkward and unmanageable rates, besides which, if stock had been created to a greater amount than the cash really received, what did it matter after all ? The Government was not bound to pay it off at par, but could always go into the market like anyone else and buy it at the price of the day, and if the price of the day should be higher than the price of issue, it only showed that the credit of the nation had improved, which would be a matter to rejoice over and not to cavil at ; as the stock, moreover, was held in England by Englishmen, its redemption at a higher rate was, to a certain extent, but a transference from one pocket to another, and was no loss to the country as a whole. It would be beside our purpose to follow this argument any further, and I only referred to it in order to explain the growth of Consols, for as it was in the Three percents, that most of the loans raised at the time were funded, the stock increased in the 30 years between 1776 and 1805 from 38 millions to 390 millions, or at the rate of over 11 millions a year. Great reductions were afterwards made, but it still amounted in 1888 to 323 millions. In that year the famous stock which had endured for 136 years, and which had triumphantly withstood the assaults of Mr. Gladstone and Mr. Childers, finally succumbed to the determined attack of Mr. Goschen, and the "sweet simplicity of the Three percents" is now a thing of the past.

LONDON DAILY STOCK AND SHARE LIST.

THIRD LECTURE.

[Delivered 24 January 1898.]

I HAVE already had occasion to mention that the old Three per-cent Consols reached par thrice during the last half-century, and that on each occasion the guardian of our public purse had felt it his duty to try and drive a somewhat harder bargain with the national creditor. Two of these attempts—the conversions of 1853 and 1880—ended, as we know, in failure, Mr. Gladstone being defeated by unfavourable politics, and Mr. Childers by the opposition of the city; but the scheme put forward by Mr. Goschen in 1888 met with general acceptance and was triumphantly carried through. His plan was simplicity itself. He offered the holders of the Three per-cents (New, Reduced, and Consols), a new stock, at par, bearing 3 per-cent for one year and $2\frac{3}{4}$ per-cent for 14 years, until April 1903; after which the rate fell automatically to $2\frac{1}{2}$ per-cent, but was guaranteed against any further reduction until 1923. (It may be remarked in passing, that, in comparing the price with others, it will be found simpler to regard the new Consols as a Two-and-a-Half per-cent stock, and to deduct the present value of the $\frac{1}{4}$ per-cent bonus from the price. Thus, if you deduct $1\frac{1}{4}$, the approximate present value of a five years' bonus of $\frac{1}{4}$ per-cent from to-day's quotation of $112\frac{3}{4}$, you get $111\frac{1}{2}$ as the price of a Two-and-a-Half per-cent stock).

The phenomenal success of the conversion is to be ascribed to the favour with which it was received by the banking interest, who, knowing that the reduction was bound to come sooner or later, and finding on examination that the scheme contained all the good points, and none of the bad ones, of its predecessors, consented to lead the way, and were followed by the public. In the first place, instead of contracting the market by splitting up existing stocks, Mr. Goschen proposed to enlarge it by merging the whole of the Three per-cents into one great and homogeneous stock, which would amount to between five and six hundred millions; secondly, there were no alternatives to puzzle the investor, or arouse his suspicion—one stock alone was offered, and he must either take that or his money; thirdly, no book-keeping complications were created by disturbance of capital—£100 old stock exchanged for £100 new stock, neither more nor less; and lastly, Mr. Goschen proposed to retain the time-honoured name of Consols by giving his new creation the title of Two-and-Three-quarters per-cent *Consolidated* Stock. As to the first point—the preference shown for a large, instead of a small, stock,—I may explain that the banker looks on Consols from a point of view somewhat different from that of the ordinary investor, who is attracted mainly by their absolute safety. The security they offer—that of a first mortgage on the whole of the national assets—is, of course, the best conceivable. No promise or obligation whatever is, or can be, so good as the bond of a great, wealthy, and honourable nation. Railway Debentures and Corporation Stocks rank next in order; but it is quite conceivable that railways may some day be ruined by the invention of a new mode of locomotion, whilst a great conflagration or the collapse of some particular industry might render the bond of a city almost worthless. But the taxability of the British nation is all but inexhaustible. We can augment the national income, if need be, in a manner and to an extent which no other community or corporation possibly can, and on that income the service of the debt is the first charge. In addition, however, to this indispensable quality of perfect security, the banker requires something else. He also requires the scarcely less valuable attribute of convertibility—of convertibility, that is to say, without delay, and at a minimum of expense or loss. Next to cash in his reserves, he ranks such securities as are immediately realizable in time of difficulty or pressure, and repeated experience has shown him that, in this respect, Consols stand first and alone, because owing to their magnitude they offer at all times a free market, and a market, moreover, in which the dealer's "turn" and the broker's commission are cut down to the very lowest figures. As you see from the quotation, the "turn of the market" is only $\frac{1}{8}$ per-cent, and is the lowest of any stock in the List. As a matter of fact, the jobbers in that market will always make you a $\frac{1}{8}$ price, and under pressure, might even quote a $\frac{1}{16}$ price, and as Consols are changing hands daily and hourly in all imaginable sums, they constitute a stock which the banker can get in and out of both easily and cheaply. There is but one article known to commerce of which we are able to say positively that at all times and under all circumstances you can be certain of instantly turning it into cash in London, and that is—gold; but next to gold in the quality of ready saleability comes Consols, and it is no exaggeration to say that on a day of panic it would be easier to sell half-a-million of them than it would be to find a buyer for fifty thousand pounds' worth of Indian or Colonial Stock, or of Railway Debentures. Another prepossessing feature of the new stock was, as I mentioned, its name. Care had to be taken that the appellation should not clash with that of Mr. Childers' Two-and-Three-quarters per-cents, and in bestowing on it the title of Consolidated Stock, Mr. Goschen expressed a hope that, after the extinction of the Three per-cents, the public would transfer to it the old and familiar abbreviation of "Consols." That hope was fulfilled; but Mr. Goschen had a very narrow escape from being immortalized, for in the neck-and-neck struggle that ensued between "Consols" and "Goschens" for popular favour, it certainly looked for a time as though the latter were to be the winner. There appears to be no previous instance of the word "stock" being employed in the official designation of any part of the Funded Debt, and, to a certain extent, it is a misnomer. The root is that of the verb "stick", and the primary notion is that of something which is stuck in and remains fast. The fund contributed by those who took shares in the first public companies, such as the East India Company, the Bank of England, the South Sea Company, &c., was called the "Capital *Stock*", probably because the money when once put in could not be taken out again, and the term appears to have been applied by analogy to the imaginary capital of the Government Annuities. This view of the case appears to have been taken by Richardson in his New English Dictionary (1844), where he describes stocks as "the public funds where the money of unhappy persons is now fixed." Our finances were at a very low ebb in 1844, and that might explain the definition. The profit, too, that was periodically divided by such companies was called the "dividend"; and by carrying the analogy a step further, the instalments periodically paid by Government on account of the Perpetual Annuities were also called dividends.

Having just referred to the principal sum, in respect of which the Perpetual Annuities are payable, as an "imaginary capital", it would, perhaps, be well to be a little more explicit. The National Debt divides, as we have seen, into two branches, between which it is now necessary to draw a very sharp distinction. The one—the Unfunded or Floating Debt—actually *is* debt, being made up of obligations to pay certain definite sums of money on certain fixed days; but the other, the so-called Funded Debt, is really no debt at all. That um of five hundred and odd millions which you see standings in the List as the present amount of Consols, was never borrowed by the Government; the money is not owing to anybody; and the State has never promised to pay it to anybody. What happened was this. The Government, wishing on various occasions to raise money for certain purposes, created Perpetual Annuities of £3 each, and *sold* them, at the best price obtainable, in sufficient quantity to realize the sum required. The thing sold was a perpetual annuity; that is to say, an unending series of future annual payments of £3 each; and the price given for it was a lump sum of money down, which, whether £100, or whether only £50, was, all things considered, of equal value at the time of payment. Strictly speaking, there was no question of a loan in the transaction at all, but only of a purchase and sale. If I were to buy a £5 life annuity from an insurance company for £100, I presume you would regard it as nonsense to say that the company *owed* me £100; and, in like manner, it is irrational to suppose, because I buy a Perpetual Government Annuity of 55s., that the Government actually owes me £100, on which it has undertaken to pay me 2¾ per-cent interest. The only engagement it enters into is an engagement to pay me a specific annuity, and, so long as that annuity is duly forthcoming, it does not owe me a penny. I have not told you quite the whole of the bargain, however. As the State might, some day, wish to pay off the annuitant, it always took care to stipulate that, after a certain date, and after giving a certain notice, it should have the right to buy back the annuity at the fixed price of £100. The price the Government got for it made no matter; whether they had sold it cheap just before Waterloo, or sold it dear just after, was all one; if they ever wanted to dispossess the holder of it against his will, they undertook to give him £100. Mr. Goschen made precisely the same stipulation nine years ago. Here is what he said in "'The National Debt (Conversion) Act, 1888'": "The new stock shall "not be redeemable until the fifth day of April, one thousand "nine hundred and twenty-three, but on and after that day "shall be redeemable by Parliament on such notice, at such "time or times, and either in one sum, or in such sums or "proportions, and in such order and manner as Parliament "may direct, at the rate of one hundred pounds sterling for "every one hundred pounds of the capital sums in respect of "which the annuities constituting the stock are payable." While all else about the redemption has been left to the future discretion of Parliament, the price at which it shall take place is definite and unmistakeable. What we are to understand by the statement in the List that the present amount of Consolidated Stock is £525,000,000 is now growing clearer. That sum is not debt; for Consolidated Stock is merely the name given to a huge mass of perpetual annuities, and so long as the quarterly instalments are punctually met, there can be nothing owing. It is simply the maximum redemption-value—the outside limit of the sum we may be called upon to pay in case the holder of the annuity refuses to part with it until he is forced. But, in addition, there also attaches to it a conventional signification, based, not on principle, but on general agreement and custom. Whether you regard £2. 15s. as the amount of an annuity, pure and simple, or whether, for convenience in book-keeping and to avoid a troublesome circumlocution, you choose to consider it as the annual interest on a hypothetical principal of £100, makes little difference when once you are quite clear as to the true nature of the bargain; and, as a matter of fact, it has been found extremely convenient, both by the State and the annuitant, to adopt the latter supposition. The old consols were not called annuities of £3 each, but annuities of £3 *per-cent* each, and the "per-cent" referred to an imaginary capital of £100 which the Government assigned to each of them, with a view, no doubt, to simplify the keeping of the accounts. It was not necessary to do so; and the French Consols (Rentes) which resemble ours, make no mention at all of a principal. A certificate of French Rente states the amount of the annual payment to which the bearer is entitled, but says nothing about a capital sum. Yet, even the French are illogical; for, though they studiously avoid all mention of a capital sum, they, at the same time, entitle the stock Three *per-cent* Rente. The Government, I said, assigned a hypothetical principal of £100 to each annuity; and when we speak of buying or selling £100 Consols, we really mean the annuity corresponding to an imaginary capital of £100 stock. I trust you will now understand, therefore, that "Funded *Debt*", "borrowing", or "raising a loan" (as applied to a fresh issue of consols), and such like expressions, though sanctioned by ordinary usage, must be taken strictly in a conventional, and not in too literal a sense.

Let us now turn our attention to "The National Debt Act, 1870", which regulates the transfer and dividend arrangements of all the Funds, and which, being a consolidation of the various enactments relating to the perpetual annuities that had been making their appearance on the Statute Book at greater or less intervals ever since the end of the seventeenth century, presents matter of interest that we cannot afford to overlook. It was passed, of course, before the Two-and-Three-quarters per-cents, and the new Consols were created, but the Acts of 1884 and 1888 both incorporate its provisions by reference. The first section that appears to call for special comment is No. 7, which says—"The annuities and dividends aforesaid " shall continue to be free from all taxes, charges, and im- " positions, in like manner as heretofore." Now, I think it probable that if I were to ask any one of you to put your own rational construction on that clause, and to tell me what it meant, you would be inclined to reply that it was so clearly expressed in plain English as to need no interpretation, and that it just meant what it distinctly said, namely, that the dividends on consols and on the other perpetual annuities shall be payable free from all taxes, as hitherto. But, if that be the true meaning, how comes it that the dividends are not actually paid free from all taxes? How comes it that the Bank of England deducts income tax; and that, if your quarterly dividend be £10, the Bank keeps back 6s. 8d., and only gives you £9. 13s. 4d. To the legal mind there may appear to be no inconsistency in that deduction, but to us, who have not had the benefit of a legal training, it certainly seems to call for explanation; and, in order that we may view the matter in a right light, we will ask, firstly, with what object that clause could have been incorporated in the original Loan Acts, and secondly, whether the imposition of income tax on the dividends is, or is not, consistent with the spirit and purpose of the exemption. As to its purpose there can be little doubt. It was meant to protect the fundholder from sharp practice on the part of the Government. The lender of money to the State had in view the possibility that, at some time or other an unwise or unscrupulous Minister might attempt to trick him out of part of his money under the pretext of taxation; and he therefore stipulated that payment of the full annuity, without deduction, should be one of the terms of the bargain. The other question is more difficult to answer. To judge whether or no the imposition of income tax is a violation of contract we shall have to glance at the circumstances under which it was originally levied. The first Income Tax Act was passed in 1799, a few years after we had entered into the great war. The impost was sanctioned because there was no help for it. Money had to be raised by hook or by crook, and however obnoxious a tax of such an oppressive and inquisitorial nature might be, no other way could be found of raising it. *All* income, from whatever source it might be derived, was made chargeable, and whether the taxpayer obtained his revenue from trading or from a profession, from landed property or from funded property, made no difference. In one case as in another it was income, and as such had to pay; and though no special mention was made in the Act of the public funds, yet as all the dividends formed part of somebody's receipts they, of course, contributed in common with other income. Shortly afterwards, on the renewal of the tax, a change was made in the manner of its collection, the principle being adopted, which we still adhere to, of charging incomes *at their source*, that is to say, of charging them when in the hands of the first possessor, instead of in the hands of the ultimate proprietor.

The tax on rent, for instance, was to be collected from the occupier instead of the landlord; the tax on interest, from the borrower instead of the lender; and the tax on income derived from the funds, instead of being gathered from the fundholder himself, was to be collected from the Bank of England, which was authorised to deduct it from the dividends. All at once the fundholder discovered that his annuity was no longer payable free from all taxes. "You have broken faith with me," he cried. "You pledged your "solemn word to pay me without deduction, and now you "begin to violate the compact!" "Nothing of the sort!" indignantly retorted Mr. Pitt. "I only promised that no tax "should be imposed on the stockholder, separately and "distinctly. I only promised that no impost should be "levelled directly at the fundholder, as such, and I still "uphold that promise in its integrity. The engagement was "sacred, and whatever happens, we will stand by it. We "tax the dividend, *not as dividend, but as income;* and so long "as we subject it to no special tax, but treat it only like all "other income, we maintain that your exemption remains "inviolate." Now, who was right? Was the fundholder or was Mr. Pitt? I express no opinion; but simply tell you how the imposition was justified. Mark, however, the result of setting a bad example. Section 71 of our Act says—"No "stamp duty shall be payable in respect of any dividend "warrant, transfer of stock, stock certificate, or coupon," which is language as unequivocal as it well can be. Nevertheless, in 1831, Lord Althorp proposed to levy a duty of ½ per-cent on all transfers of stock, and when the astonished House reminded him of this express provision in all the Loan Acts, calmly asserted that his proposal could not possibly be construed into a breach of faith, inasmuch as he intended charging *all* transfers, and not transfers of the funds alone, which, to his mind, appeared precisely on all fours with the precedent set by Mr. Pitt. So great, however, was the outburst of anger which the scheme provoked that it was at once withdrawn. Then again, in 1852 Mr. Disraeli proposed to tax income from the funds at a higher rate than other income, which likewise would have been a clear violation of principle. Immediately the war was over the tax had to be taken off, and I may mention, as an interesting scrap of history, that, in order to be rid of the detested impost once for all, the

House ordered the assessment papers and the records of the Commissioners' proceedings to be destroyed, and was very near falling in with Mr. Brougham's serio-jocular suggestion that they should be publicly burnt by the common hangman. After that, though successive administrations cast many a longing look on the forbidden tax, over a quarter of a century passed before any minister could summon up sufficient courage to propose its re-imposition, and it was only under a very grave sense of the disaster threatening our national finances that Sir Robert Peel dared to do so in 1842. Desperate diseases justify desperate remedies; but the remedy in this case, I am sorry to say, overstepped the limits of national probity. During the former continuance of the income tax, Mr. Pitt had carefully laid down and maintained one great distinction, which he justly considered essential to public faith, namely, the exemption from its incidence of foreign fund-holders residing abroad, who, as they were not represented in Parliament, could not be said to have accepted the tax through the vote of their spokesman, as might have been argued in the case of the British fundholder. Foreigners residing in this country, and enjoying the protection of its government and laws, are bound to pay their share of the expense of keeping up that protection, but, as there exists neither the power nor the right to impose British taxes on foreigners residing outside our dominions, it is clear that, if taxed at all, they are taxed as fundholders, and as fundholders only. But Mr. Pitt contended that he was not taxing the fundholder, as such, and, as a logical sequence of that contention, he exempted the foreign holder. Sir Robert Peel, on the other hand, decided not to exempt him; and, it is difficult to arrive at any other conclusion but that, in so doing, he committed a breach of good faith. The chief reason alleged for the departure from precedent was that exemption might open the door to fraud, by inducing British subjects to register their stock in foreign names, but even if evasion of the tax had been an established fact, instead of a mere assumption, it would have been no justification for paying the foreigner less than we had promised to pay him, or, in other words, for partial repudiation. To defend the imposition is, in short, tantamount to asserting that those who have borrowed money shall be at liberty to tax the lenders at their own discretion, which is preposterous. The only extenuating circumstance—

and a lame excuse it is—that we can now plead for neglecting
to reverse Sir Robert Peel's decision, is that all aliens who, at
the present time, hold British funds, have acquired them
subject to that condition. The course taken by Sir Robert
Peel was not only a violation of contract, it was also a blunder.
It was pointed out to him that the national obligations of
many countries were almost entirely in the hands of foreigners
—principally Englishmen—and that if England once set the
fashion of taxing debt, it would be difficult to blame them for
imitating us, as they assuredly would. That warning we have
since had reason to remember, and may have again. Italy,
for instance, takes toll from all holders of her Rente, and
India taxes the dividend on rupee paper, and a few years
ago I remember noticing that a prominent colonial statesman
had been advocating the imposition of income tax on New
Zealand stocks. The British bondholder, he argued, had
a direct interest in the maintenance of order and good
government in the colony, and might help to pay for them.
I daresay you will think I am treating this question with an
unwarrantable degree of prolixity, but as there is an important
principle involved in its consideration, I wished to place it
before you as clearly as I could. Returning now to our Clause
No. 7, we can make sense of it by mentally adding " except
income tax ", or by reading it in conjunction with No. 36,
which openly recognizes the deduction. The greater part of
the rest of the Act is made up of regulations concerning the
management of the Debt. The arrangements respecting such
matters as the payment of dividends, the transfer of stock
from one person to another, the preparation of certificates, and
so forth, are not settled by voluntary agreement between the
Government and the Bank, as might be supposed, but are
prescribed by statute. The law provides, for instance, that all
the dividends shall be payable at the Bank of England—so
that, if the Chancellor of the Exchequer wanted to make part
of them payable elsewhere, he would have to get a special Act
of Parliament passed to authorize it—and it also provides
(Sec. 72) that the Bank of England shall continue a corporation
as long as any part of the Debt remains unpaid. It is, of
course, infinitely more convenient to the fundholder to be able
to draw his dividend or transfer his stock in the very heart of
the City than it would be to have to go to the Treasury or to
Somerset House for that purpose, but the original reason for

bringing in the name of the Bank was probably to convince the public that everything was straightforward about the loan, just as at the present day its name inspires confidence in, and gives a fillip to, a Colonial or Corporation issue, and that of Rothschild to a foreign one. The Act also imposes upon the Government the duty of paying over to the Chief Cashier of the Bank, out of the Consolidated Fund, sufficient money to meet the dividends as they fall due; and, if there should not be enough standing to its credit at the time, it is empowered by the Exchequer and Audit Act of 1866 to borrow the difference from the Bank, on condition of repaying it from the first accruing revenue of the next quarter. The operation of these provisions is to make the dividends on the Public Debt, when they become due, a charge upon the moneys in the Exchequer in priority to all other claims; and, in the event of the sum being insufficient, a prior charge is created upon the first receipts of revenue thereafter. As to Part IV., which deals with the subject of transfer, it is obvious that, as the Debt is only repayable at the option of the Government, and that, as the stockholder's title consists simply of an entry in the books of the Bank, and not of a document (the so-called stock receipt which the purchaser receives, merely proves that a transfer in his name was effected on a certain day, beyond which it has no actual value, and is not evidence of title) capitalists would be unwilling to lend, unless there existed an easy, cheap, and speedy means of transferring their claim to someone else who was willing to buy it from them; and the Act therefore makes arrangements to that effect. The fund-holder may transfer his holding to as many people as he chooses, and the Bank will prepare the documents and make all the necessary entries without charging him a farthing for its labour, and without putting him to any trouble beyond asking him, if not personally known to them, to show that he is the party he represents himself to be (which he usually proves by getting his broker or solicitor to identify him.) No limit is imposed as to the amount that may be transferred, for as it is a great advantage to a nation that its public debt should be as much divided among the population as possible —the greater the number of State creditors, the greater being also the number of those who have a direct interest in upholding the Government—accounts may be opened for any amount from a penny upwards. I am not aware that there is any instance of an account being opened for a penny, but I believe there are cases where people have transferred nearly the whole of their stock and carelessly left a trifle over, so that there are accounts standing over in the Bank's books for a few pence. And now we will leave the Act.

The best of all instruments, it has sometimes been said, for the discovery of truth in political economy, is a reference to like circumstances or to similar transactions in private life; and one of the applications of this principle supplies a favourite argument to debt reformers. " What should we think," they ask, "of the moral courage of a private individual who, in " bad years, or whenever he had exceptional expenditure to " meet, made a practice of borrowing money on the mortgage " of his estate ; but who, instead of striving in good years to " clear off the encumbrance, allowed his opportunities to slip " by, and accustomed himself to regard the burden as a " dispensation of Providence, which it was useless to struggle " against. If such conduct would be contemptible in the " individual, how can it be otherwise than reprehensible in the " case of that aggregate of individuals which we call a nation." It is quite conceivable, they admit, that, if the estate were undergoing development, it might be good policy to let the mortgage stand and to lay out all the money that could be spared in improvements, which, in after years, might return ten-fold; but, when once its productive powers are fully evolved, and when the annual yield becomes greater than the amount that can be wisely spent again upon it, then prudence and common sense dictate that the proprietor should address himself seriously to the task of paying off the mortgage. That is one side of the question ; now let us hear what can be argued on the other. In the first place, it is maintained that, as the public creditor is our fellow-citizen, and that, as a debt owing by one part of the community to another is, in a national sense, no debt at all, it is just as absurd to be alarmed at the magnitude of the sum owing by the public debtor as it would be to take fright at the total of, let us say, our banking deposits, which are also money owing by one part of the community to another. The interest paid on the debt is national expenditure, and has to be provided for by taxation, true !—but it is also national income, and helps to pay that taxation; and though the Chancellor of the Exchequer takes money from us with one hand to meet the debt charge, yet he gives it back with the other in the shape of the quarterly dividends. If the National Debt, in fact, were paid off to-morrow, the nation would not be a penny the richer, except as regards the smaller portion of it held by foreigners, and, indeed, if anything, it would even be poorer, for a part of the dislodged capital would inevitably be exchanged for some of the rubbish of the stock and share market, and its owners never see it back. This, in the main is true ; and, at any rate, there is no gainsaying the fact that the weight of a debt held at home, as consols and French rentes are, and of which the interest is spent at home, is not nearly so much felt as that of a debt held abroad, and the interest upon which has to be sent out of the country. Nevertheless, even an internal debt is an evil, and that for at least three reasons : (1) A great deal of money is wasted over the operation of raising the interest, the nation having to support an army of tax-gatherers, many of whom, if the debt were extinguished, could be better employed otherwise; (2) The interest, added to our necessary expenditure, tends to use up the good and fair taxes, and to leave us, in case of war, with only the unjust and irritating taxes to fall back upon; (3) While the whole community, from A to Z, must contribute to make up the interest, only a small portion of it, only A, B, and C, receive that interest. Another argument against redemption is that the national creditors, as a body, do not ask or wish to be paid, but on the contrary, strenuously object. Whenever a holder, here or there, wants to have his money back, there is always someone else ready to buy him out, and step into his place. Then, again, the funds are the one investment that is absolutely safe, and that requires no looking after ; the one investment which widows and orphans, and all those who are incapable of the business-like management of property, may put their money into, and sleep in peace, and the one investment into which bankers can place their reserves with the certainty of being able to realize whenever necessary. Lastly, the money to repay debt must in part— not all, but in part—be withdrawn from profitable occupation. Whilst the debt subsists, the public creditor is virtually advancing capital to the public debtor at a little over 2½ per-cent, or including all expenses of collection and management, at say 3 per-cent, and the latter can employ that capital to yield him double or treble as much. By redeeming its indebtedness, therefore, the nation ceases to pay interest on the amount discharged, but ceases also to receive profit on the money so applied, or rather, on that portion of the money so applied which was previously laid out to advantage. In spite, however, of these and such like plausible and ingenious arguments, the general opinion—and certainly the opinion of those whose judgment is entitled to the greatest respect—is that a generation whose taxes are light, productive, and unimpeding, ought undoubtedly to do something to ease the burden of coming generations, which can hardly be much better off than we are and may be a great deal worse off. Our children and our children's children will have their own exigencies to provide for, and it is our plain duty, in time of national well-being and prosperity, to work off a part of our great mortgage, and not to hand down to them difficulties which it is in our power to alleviate. We must remember, too, that the faster we pay off debt the better our credit, and that our credit is what we rely upon for help in time of trouble. If England should again become involved in a great and protracted struggle—and who shall say that we may not? —it is no exaggeration to say that two or three years of war expenditure on the modern scale would probably suffice to re-add to the debt the reductions of a century.

The first Minister to establish a fund for the redemption of the Debt, and the first Minister, also, to lay violent hands on the accumulation, as soon as it became worth the stealing, was Sir Robert Walpole; but the Sinking Fund which is best remembered is that established by Pitt in 1786. This was based practically on the amazing principle, that if the nation lent itself money, charged itself interest, and continually invested and re-invested that interest in fresh loans to itself, it would, in course of time, grow so rich that the Debt could be paid off with the utmost ease, and yet nobody be a penny the poorer. The House and the country were delighted with the plan, and it passed by acclamation. Some stupid people —people of that sort who always try to pick holes in what they cannot understand—said it was repugnant to common sense to suppose that the nation could gain riches by lending to itself, any more than a shopkeeper could make money by buying his own stock; but it was explained to them how a certain Dr. Price had calculated that if one penny had been put out at our Saviour's birth at five per-cent compound interest, it would, by the year 1781, have increased to a greater sum than would be contained in two hundred million globes, the size of the earth, all of solid gold, while, at simple interest, it would in the same time have amounted to no more than seven shillings and sixpence. "Well", said the disbelievers, " and what of that"? "Why, simply this", was the triumphant reply. "Let the Chancellor of the Exchequer *borrow* a million a year at *simple* interest, and *lend* a million a year at *compound* interest, and—there you are"! This arithmetical puzzle deluded the nation for years, and throughout the whole of the French war we kept up the farce of annually paying off large sums of debt, though we always borrowed the money with which to pay it, and a great deal more besides. Mr. Pitt himself was not deceived. There is no doubt that he really meant to redeem the debt out of savings; but that, finding this impossible, and having to choose between either a fictitious Sinking Fund, or none at all, he deliberately adopted the former alternative, in the hope that, by educating the country to regard reduction of debt as a bounden duty, he might be able, when better times came round, to change pretence into reality. Eventually, however, the nation saw its folly, and, in 1829, the whole of the previous legislation affecting the Sinking Fund was swept away. In its stead was instituted the sound and solid principle that the *actual surplus* of income over expenditure in every financial year shall be paid over to the National Debt Commissioners, and by them be applied in immediate cancellation of debt. This system, which has remained in operation down to the present day, is known as the *Old* Sinking Fund, and it may be well to point out with regard to it that the *actual* surplus in question is not to be confounded with the *estimated* surplus, which the Chancellor of the Exchequer is, now-a-days, expected to provide, and make us a present of, on Budget night. If, I repeat, there should remain, at the end of the financial year, a genuine balance to the good—not of hypothetical figures, but of actual cash—that money must, by Act of Parliament, be laid out in the payment of debt; and, as it was formerly the practice of our Finance Ministers not to count their chickens before they were hatched, by anticipating the normal growth of revenue, the Old Sinking Fund has served to effect a genuine cancellation of indebtedness to the amount, at the end of 1896, of seventy-nine millions. Until twenty-three years ago, the revenue estimates of the coming year were based strictly on the actual receipts of the previous year, without one sixpence of allowance for the augmentation that might reasonably be anticipated as a natural outcome of the growth of population; but the system came to a sudden end, under curious circumstances, in 1874, coincidently with the fall of the Liberal administration. In his appeal to the country, in the early part of that year, Mr. Gladstone had held out the bribe of a total repeal of the income tax, and had demonstrated the possibility of its abolition by a sort of *pro-formâ* Budget statement, in which he took into account the full normal expansion of revenue; but, though the electors refused to take Mr. Gladstone back, they hungered after the surplus which he had dangled before their eyes, and when the Conservatives took office, they deemed it expedient not to disappoint the country in that respect, but to adopt the estimates of their predecessors. In this way the system was initiated, which has ever since prevailed, of discounting the elasticity of the revenue by estimates which are drawn up with scientific precision, and which aim at the closest possible approach to perfect accuracy. If we make estimates at all, it is, doubtless, better that they should be true ones; but, for all that, financial reformers look back with regret to the years 1865 to 1874, during which, by wilfully under-estimating our income, we were able to wipe off debt to the amount of many millions. Having deprived the "Old Sinking Fund" of its virtue, Sir Stafford Northcote was bound, in common decency, to take other measures for the liquidation of debt, as it was quite obvious that popular pressure for the reduction of inconvenient taxation would never allow him to put aside an *estimated* surplus for that purpose. We may be very virtuous and very sincere in our professions; but whenever the Chancellor of the Exchequer has money over, and asks what he shall do with it, we invariably discover that it would be a pity to waste it in paying debts. In 1875, accordingly, Sir Stafford Northcote brought forward a proposal for a "*New* Sinking Fund", which was to operate in conjunction with the existing scheme. His plan, which was simplicity itself, was to take the debt charge in the estimate of expenditure at a fixed sum, somewhat in excess of the amount actually required, and to apply the surplus each year in the purchase of consols, &c. This permanent annual charge now amounts to £25,000,000; of which about £8,000,000 represent capital, and £17,000,000 interest and cost of management. If not tampered with, it will necessarily become more effective every year. A third way—perhaps the best of all—of paying off the debt still remains; and that is, by the gradual conversion of perpetual annuities into terminable annuities. So long as we go on paying interest only, we make little progress; but, if we could add the principal to the interest, and pay the two together by means of fixed annual instalments extending over a term of years, the time would eventually come when both would disappear. This plan was always open to us; but the objection to it was its costliness, as people could not be induced to buy terminable annuities, unless the price was disproportionately low. They were disliked for several reasons. The proper way to deal with them is to re-invest each year a certain part of the annual income, so that, at the termination of the annuity you may have entire the sum you spent in buying it; but most persons do not know how to make the necessary calculations, and the ordinary investor—if he is wise—avoids what he cannot understand. Then, again, as the tendency of Government stock is to rise, and as the amount to be paid for a terminable annuity was always based on the current price of consols at the time of the sale, there was ever a possibility that the annual re-investment would prove insufficient to replace the capital. Lastly, income tax had to be paid on the full amount of the annuity—both on the capital and interest—and, if the tax went up, the holder might find himself a good deal out in his estimate. The consequence was that, though the system of terminable annuities (or long annuities, as we formerly called them) has been in existence even longer than the Funded Debt—the first loan on this basis having been issued in 1692—they were never a favourite form of investment, and those in existence up to 1860 had, in most cases, been forced out by the custom of the Government, when raising money, of granting, in addition to the stock created, bonuses in the form of terminable annuities. Shortly after the establishment of the Post Office Savings' Bank in 1861, it occurred, however, to Mr. Gladstone, that if he created large blocks of annuities in his capacity of Chancellor of the Exchequer, he might himself purchase them in his capacity of custodian of the poor man's savings. It occurred to him that, as he was the largest fundholder on the books, he might, from time to time, commute portions of the stock held by him against Savings

Banks' funds into terminable annuities, and, by thus increasing the present burden of the nation, diminish its future burden. The plan worked, and has continued to work, admirably. In 1883, no less than £70,000,000 of Consols, £30,000,000 of which belonged to the Savings Banks' Fund, and £40,000,000 to the Chancery Paymaster, were in this way cancelled, and terminable annuities set up to replace the Stock. Let me explain again what the scheme is. The Chancellor of the Exchequer sent, we will suppose, for the Paymaster-General of the Court of Chancery, and said: "I want to make a " proposal to you. I find that you are the holder of " £40,000,000 of stock, which you hold as an investment, " and which you will, no doubt, continue to hold for the next " twenty years. If you will hand that stock over to me to be " cancelled, I will give you, in exchange, a twenty years' " annuity of £2,666,000. Of this amount, £1,200,000 repre- " sents the interest you have hitherto been receiving, so " that, as far as that item goes, you are just in the same " position as though you kept the stock, and the remaining " £1,466,000 represents return of capital, which, if annually " invested by you in Consols, and allowed to accumulate, will, " in twenty years' time, reinstate you in possession of your " £40,000,000 of stock." These terminable annuities are, at present, automatically paying off upwards of £4,500,000 a-year, and, in case of emergency, we always have the convenient option of re-converting them into an equivalent amount of stock—a process which, though it amounts to the same thing as suspension of the sinking fund, does not sound quite so alarming. The total amount paid off by the sinking fund system is continually on the increase, and, at the present time, is about £8,000,000 a-year. Assuming that the State can borrow at 2½ per-cent (it can actually borrow at much less), that sum would pay the interest on a capital of £320,000,000 ; so that, by simply suspending the sinking fund, England could raise a war loan of £300,000,000 without adding a single shilling to the taxation of the country. Other nations, who boast of *their* war-chests, might mark that fact with advantage. Now, as it is obvious, on consideration, that every mode of alleviating the burden of debt must resolve itself, under whatever name it may be known, into the appro-priation, to that end, of *actual surplus revenue*, and nothing more, the question suggests itself—Why should it be necessary to hide away so plain a process behind all this hocus-pocus of sinking funds and terminable annuities, as though they were ashamed of it? Why cannot Sir M. Hicks-Beach come down to the House next April and say, in a straightforward way, that our actual expenses for next year will amount to, let us say, £100,000,000, but that he means to make us pay £108,000,000, and to use the difference in writing down our liabilities for the benefit of posterity? Well, if he did, I suppose he would render himself the most unpopular man in the country. The "unemployed" would burn him in effigy, I dare say, and he would probably need police protection. The fact is that, in matters of this sort, it is expedient—nay, more than expedient, it is necessary—to hoodwink the country. Experience has proved, beyond all question, that Parliament cannot be trusted to deliberately vote large specific annual sums towards the repayment of debt; but that, on the other hand, if it once consents to devote a certain sum to the setting up of an annuity, it can be relied upon to keep its word, and not to be for ever tampering with the arrangement; and the more so, because, as the true nature of the operation is concealed from public view, members need not go in fear of their constituents. The complicated machinery of terminable annuities is preferable, therefore, to other methods of debt reduction, because it enables the Chancellor of the Exchequer to make sure that our efforts to lighten the load that presses on the industry of the nation will be steady and unremitting in their application, and increasingly beneficial in their result. A few words with reference to the price-movements of consols will exhaust what is still left to say about them. Without going into details, I think it is possible to enunciate a general principle that will account for all their fluctuations. The law appears to be no more than this; that, if the disturbing influence of politics could be eliminated, the steady application of the New Sinking Fund, the operation of the terminable annuities, and the unceasing absorption of the stock into other channels where such holdings are a necessity, must inevitably cause a continuous upward movement. Supply being limited, the ever-present demand cannot fail, when other influences are in abeyance, to produce a perpetual enhancement of value. But consols are a *political* security; and a political occurrence of real magnitude might, as has happened before, bring down the price with startling rapidity.

Holders of the national stock appear to lose their heads over events which would hardly cause possessors of Metropolitans or of railway debenture stocks to turn a hair, and the reason is not far to seek. It is not because our credit begins to totter immediately a war-cloud is seen on the horizon; on the contrary, our credit is stability itself; and, since 1815, no public annuitant has ever, for an instant, doubted the safety of his investment. It is because Consols are a stock the quantity of which is liable to indefinite and absolutely incalculable expansion. In the event of our becoming involved in a first-class war, the quantity forced on the market might reckon, not by millions, but by scores—even hundreds—of millions; and the greater the augmentation of supply, the greater the depreciation of value. That is why "bulls" of the stock are in such a hurry to scuttle out whenever politics take an unfavourable turn, and why the public also, if matters look really serious, become anxious to part with their holdings at a small present loss, in order to avoid the possibility of a greater future sacrifice.

LONDON DAILY STOCK AND SHARE LIST.

FOURTH LECTURE.

[Delivered 7 February 1898.]

WHEN speaking the other evening of the Two-and-a-half per-cent Stock originally created by Mr. Gladstone in 1854, I mentioned the fact that both Mr. Childers and Mr. Goschen had referred to its importance as a testing machine by which to ascertain the true value of the public credit, and it has since occurred to me that it would be of interest to further elucidate this point, by instituting a comparison between the present prices and the yield of Consols, Local Loans Stock, and the Two-and-a-half per-cents, all of which, being based on exactly the same security, ought, after allowance is made for the difference in the dates of redemption, to give about the same return. Consols are redeemable in 1923, Local Loans Stock in 1912, and the Two-and-a-half per-cents in 1905, and we shall assume, in each instance, that the holder will be paid off at par at these respective dates, which is the worst that can happen to him. In each case we must, of course, deduct accrued interest from the price, and, as all the stocks stand over par, we must also in each case, set up an annuity which, if allowed to accumulate at $2\frac{1}{2}$ per-cent until the date of redemption, will, by that time, restore the premium which the buyer at to-day's price would otherwise lose.

Price of Consols		£112	12	6
Less 2 months' accrued interest		0	9	2

	£112	3	4

Less the present value of a 5 years' annuity of 5s., deducted in order to reduce the stock to a 2½ percent basis 1 3 4

Net price ...	£111	0	0

Gross yield... ... ... £2 10 0
Less amount of annual sinking fund necessary to replace the premium of £11 at end of 25 years 0 6 5

Net yield	£2	3	7

If £111 yield 2 3 7
£100 will yield 1 19 3

Price of Local Loans Stock £113 10 0
Less 2 months' accrued interest 0 10 0

£113 0 0

Gross yield... ... ... £3 0 0
Less annual sinking fund to replace £13 at end of 14 years 0 15 9

Net yield ... £2 4 3
If £113 yield 2 4 3
£100 will yield 1 19 2

Price of Two-and-a-half per-cents ... £106 0 0
Less 2 months' accrued interest ... 0 8 4

£105 11 8

Gross yield... ... ... £2 10 0
Less annual sinking fund to replace £5 11 8 at end of 7 years ...   0 14 9

Net yield ... £1 15 3
If £105 11 8 yield ...   1 15 3
£100 will yield 1 13 5

This remarkable result can only be explained by the supposition that the cost of the Two-and-a-half per-cents "looks cheap" as compared with that of Consols and Local Loans Stock, and has induced buyers to pay what is, really, an extravagant price. If we reject this explanation, the only inference open to us is, that the true value of British credit is less than 1¾ per-cent. We have now disposed of all the stocks constituting the National Debt, and the next item on the Official List is Local Loans Stock, the capital of which, amounting to forty-one millions, represent advances made by the State, for sundry purposes, to local authorities. The principle of lending public money to municipalities, and other corporate bodies, can be traced back for upwards of a hundred years; but, as a definite system, it took shape in 1817, when, owing to the disorganization of the labour market, caused by the great influx of disbanded soldiers and sailors on the close of the great war, it was found necessary to start relief-works for the alleviation of distress. The system took firm root, and since that time the Government has been in the habit of making advances, through the agency of commissioners, for almost every conceivable purpose—for sanitary and water works; for schools, free libraries, and artizans' dwellings; for harbours and lighthouses; for markets and fairs; and so forth—the object in view being to assist small communities who desire to carry out really useful works, but who, although they may have fairly good security to offer, could hardly borrow in the open market without great disadvantage, because the amounts they require are so small. During the past thirty or forty years in particular, great extension has been given to this plan of borrowing from the State by numerous Acts of Parliament, which expressly authorize and encourage it. Some of these have been local Acts, passed for the purpose of enabling a particular borough to raise money for a specific object, but others, especially "The Artizans' Dwelling Act", "The Elementary Education Act", and "The Public Health Acts", have bestowed such powers on local bodies all over the country. As the objects for which such bodies are invited to incur debt are mostly matters of Imperial concern, and have been enforced by Imperial legislation, it is but just and proper that the Imperial authority should, by interposing its own credit, enable the local authority to raise the necessary funds on the best terms.

The applications for loans have to be made to certain commissioners (in England, the Public Works Loan Commissioners; in Ireland, the Board of Works and the Land Commissioners), whose business it is to ascertain whether the applicants have power to borrow, whether they have complied with the statutory provisions in regard to the loan, and whether they have sufficient security to offer. If satisfied on these points, they decide how much they will lend, and on what terms. From a recent report of the Public Works Loan Board, it appears that most of the advances have been made at $3\frac{1}{2}$ per-cent, and are repayable within thirty years; also, that fourteen millions of money are represented by balances standing at the debit of no less than 2,500 School Boards in England and Scotland, while another eight millions have been borrowed by about 1,000 Boards of Health and other sanitary authorities. Until 1887, the funds required for these advances were supplied by the Treasury, which provided the money in whatever way happened to be most convenient at the time when it was wanted. If there was plenty of cash at the bank, it simply lent from its balance; if not, it raised the means by an issue of Exchequer or Treasury Bills. As no distinction was ever made, however, between the money it borrowed to spend and that which it borrowed to lend, the National Debt had, for very many years, included a varying sum, against which there was a set-off on the other side of the account, and the Chancellor of the Exchequer used to have to explain that the debt appeared to be greater than it really was, because there were so-and-so many millions owing to the nation by local authorities which ought to be deducted. To this unsatisfactory style of book-keeping, Mr. Goschen determined, in 1887, to put an end; and he did what a merchant would have done if he found that his cashier had been lending people money against their I O U's, charging it to expenses, and re-crediting the account with it when paid back; that is to say, he ordered the general expenditure account to be entirely cleared of these items, and a separate page to be opened for them in the national ledger, in order that the country might always know exactly how it stood. The amount was thirty-seven millions, and, as a matter of course, if those millions had never been lent, the National Debt would have been that much the smaller. To complete the operation, therefore, Mr. Goschen created a new stock to the amount of thirty-seven millions, and allotted the whole of it to himself, as National Debt Commissioner, in exchange for a like total of funded and unfunded debt, which he held against savings banks' funds, and which he immediately cancelled. He also laid down the business-like principle that, whenever the local authorities wanted more money, the State was not, in future, to lend it out of its own pocket, but, if the repayments from old loans were not sufficient to meet new loans, was to *borrow* it for them; or, what came to the same thing, the State might let them have the money at once, but was invariably to recoup itself, sooner or later, by creating and selling additional issues of the new stock, to which he gave the descriptive title of Local Loans Stock. The stock was to bear 3 per-cent interest, and the difference between 3 per-cent and the rate to be charged to the local borrowers, was meant to cover expenses of management, and to provide a sinking fund for bad debts; but the money has been lent so carefully that bad debts are unknown. As regards security and exemption from stamp duty, Local Loans Stock is on precisely the same footing as Consols. Though primarily a charge on the Local Loans Fund, which consists of the interest and repayments received from the local borrowers, it is expressly provided by the Act of 1887 that any deficiency of interest shall be charged on the Consolidated Fund, and that, in default of payment by a borrower, the deficiency of capital, if any, shall be made good by Parliament. We now come to a stock which, though classed under the head of "British Funds, &c.", is in no sense a liability, either direct or indirect, of the British Government. The reason why the capital-stock of the Bank of England stands here, instead of among those of other banks, is, presumably, because "Debt due to the Bank of England" has figured as a national liability ever since we owned a funded debt, and also because bank stock for many years enjoyed the pre-eminence of being the only security, outside consols and East India stocks, in which trust funds might be invested. There is, no doubt, a very general impression that the capital of the Bank and the Government debt of eleven millions are in some way connected; and it has frequently been urged, by those who undertake the easy task of pointing out the numerous anomalies and inconsistencies of the English money market, that the State ought no longer to allow its name to appear on

the list of debtors of a trading corporation. When the debt
was originally incurred, they say, the Government was poor,
and glad to borrow, and the bank, in return for the loan of
its capital, acquired a valuable monopoly; but, as the Government is now rich, and as the bank has long ago been deprived
of its exclusive privileges, it is illogical and undignified to let
the money still be owing. Set free her capital, they argue,
and let the bank invest it in bills, and you will then see that
she will have no difficulty in rendering her control over the
market as effectual and as complete as it ought to be. Now,
this argument, plausible as it sounds, would appear to be
based on an entire misconception of the existing facts; and
those who reason in this way forget that the debt was virtually
paid off over fifty years ago. Until the Act of 1844 came
into operation, the holder of bank stock had a right to say
that the Government owed him money, for here is how the
chief cashier used to make up his balance sheet (this being
the last return issued in the old form) :

LIABILITIES.		ASSETS.	
Circulation, £21·3 millions		Securities, £22·9 millions	
Deposits ...	14·1 ,,	Bullion ... 15·6	,,
	£35·4 ,,	£38·5	,,

Only the liabilities to the public were shown, and the assets
held against them. The liabilities to the proprietors were:

Capital	...	...	...	£14·6 millions
Rest ...	...	...	...	3·1 ,,
				£17·7 ,,

and, as the Bank's other assets consisted of—

Securities	...	...	£3·6 millions
Government Debt	...		11·0 ,,
			£14·6 ,,

it is clear that the stock-holders regarded the loan to the
Government as an investment of their own money, and not of
that of the public. But the effect of the Act was to deprive
the bank of the privilege of issuing notes on its own credit,
and to convert it from a bank of issue and deposit into a

bank of deposit only. For 150 years the bank had been able to earn a large profit by issuing as many notes as it pleased against just so much cash as it pleased—and now the power to coin its credit was taken away. All notes were, henceforth, to emanate from a new Government office, called the Issue Department, the management of which was, for practical reasons, placed in the hands of the bank directors, who were, in that capacity, to act as agents of the State; and in the process of establishing that Issue Department, the Government, to all intents and purposes, discharged its debt to the bank. " You owe the note-holder twenty-one millions ", said the Chancellor of the Exchequer to the directors, " and Parlia- " ment insists that you pay him off at once. I will tell you " how to do it. You have already given me eleven millions; " now, give me ten millions more, and I will pay him off for " you, and then we can cry quits." And the bank did so. It gave the Issue Department three millions in securities, and seven millions in gold and silver, and thus got rid of its liability on the circulation. And the result was, that the eleven millions, which the Government had hitherto owed to the holders of bank stock, was henceforth to be considered as owing to the holders of issue-department notes, whom it undertakes to settle up with whenever they may feel inclined to ask for their money. Immediately afterwards, the Issue Department drew up its first balance-sheet, which was as follows :

AN ACCOUNT FOR THE WEEK ENDING 7 SEPTEMBER 1844.

Issue Department.

Notes issued £28·4 millions.	Government debt ...	£11·0	millions
	Other secu- rities ...	3·0	„
	Gold coin & bullion ...	12·7	„
	Silver bullion	1·7	„
£28·4 „		£28·4	„

This is the first account issued by the bank after the passing of the Bank Act. You will notice that the notes have increased. They were twenty-one millions in the last account, and they have increased to twenty-eight millions, because the bank itself, for its own purposes, took seven millions of the new notes. Practically, that is much the same as the account at the present day. If all these notes were presented to the bank for payment, the Government would have to intervene, because eleven millions of them are issued against the Government debt. It is clear, therefore, from this return, and from every return that has been issued subsequently, that the Government debt is really due to the note-holder, and not, as is commonly supposed, to the Governor and Company of the Bank of England, with whose trading capital it no longer has any connection whatever.

Last, though not least, of the stocks forming this group, comes the debt of our Indian Empire, the division of which into India stock and India rupee paper invites enquiry into the distinction that exists between an external and an internal loan. The essential difference between the two is, that the interest on an internal loan is payable at home, while that on an external loan has to be remitted abroad. Internal loans are those, such as consols and French rente, which a State raises in its own currency among its own subjects. External loans, on the other hand, are those which it raises in foreign currency among the inhabitants of other countries, and the interest upon which is, for the convenience of the lender, made receivable abroad. There is no reason why the native capitalist should not invest in the external debt, if he likes it better, or why the foreigner, if so inclined, should not give the preference to the obligations manufactured expressly for home consumption; but if the Calcutta merchant buys India stock, he will have to put up with the inconvenience of a certificate, the coupons attached to which are payable in London in gold, and if the London merchant buys rupee paper, he finds that the interest is payable by a draft or coupon on Calcutta for so-and-so many silver rupees. In both cases the transaction would, under present circumstances, savour more of the nature of an exchange speculation than of an investment. Another distinction is usually drawn between home and foreign loans. The one, it is said, is liable to taxation; the other not. It is held, with regard to the latter, that the borrower is bound to abide by the strict letter of his bargain, and that the terms which he imposes upon himself in the prospectus, and on the strength of which the

E

money is advanced to him, cannot afterwards be modified, unless and until he obtains the consent of the lender. Without that consent, modification is repudiation, and, as such, may entail the condign punishment of being "warned off" by the committee of the Stock Exchange. In the case of an internal loan, however, it seems to be supposed that the Government of the country is justified, seeing that it represents, at one and the same time, both fund-holder and taxpayer, in dealing with the debt in such manner as the exigencies of the State may render necessary; and that it is at full liberty to tax it, or to reduce the interest, at its own absolute discretion. But this is surely a mistake. A State which borrows money at home and then withholds from its creditors part of that which it has agreed to pay them, must be just as wanting in integrity as the State which borrows abroad and repudiates. England, it is true, taxes her home debt, and so does India; but this is explained away as a tax on income, which all pay alike; and the fact of its being universal is held to be a safeguard against injustice. In both cases, however, it is injudicious, to say the least of it, to tax the foreign holder, and, so far as India is concerned, this liability to taxation helps to explain the disparity of value between its internal and external debt obligation. If, however, instead of being an impartial tax on income derived from every source, it were a tax on income derived from the funds alone, the imposition would clearly amount to repudiation, and to repudiation in its meanest and most dangerous form. Until the year 1858, when the Government of India was transferred, after the suppression of the mutiny, from the East India Company to the Crown, rupee paper was scarcely known at all to English investors. The company had power to raise loans in this country on obtaining the sanction of Parliament; but it had usually preferred to pay a higher rate and borrow on its own authority in India, where it had contracted by far the greater part of its debt. In addition to the greater convenience and less expense of effecting interest payments on the spot, there were political reasons for the preference. The company held the wise opinion that those who had much to lose by the subversion of its power, would desire to see that power maintained; and as that astute prince, the Rajah of Chutneypore, deemed it expedient to secure the fidelity of his Sepoys by keeping their pay two or three years in arrear, so the company, on the principle that a native was a native, whether sepoy or prince, took measures to ensure the passive goodwill of His Highness by inviting him politely, but firmly, to subscribe a good round sum to their new loan. That principle still holds good in India. The home debt was practically in the shape of promissory notes, which were not capable of being held out of the country, because it was necessary to present them at the Indian Treasuries to encash the interest as it fell due. With a view to improve its credit by the removal of this obstacle, the Indian Government decided, in November 1858, to pay the interest in London by means of sight drafts on India, and issued the following notification: "When holders of notes in Calcutta desire that " the interest thereon should be made payable by bills issued " in London, they must present their notes at the office of the " Accountant-General to the Government of India, where an " enfacement* will be made on each of the notes in question, " as follows: ' Interest payable in London by draft on Calcutta " ' (or Madras, as the case may be).' " The measure was not adopted without some misgivings, as it was feared that, if the European capitalist stepped in, the native capitalist might step out, and the Indian Government thus lose its hold over the self-interest of the moneyed classes. In the result, however, the fear proved unfounded. The demand that immediately sprang up on this side for rupee paper, which returned the buyer 5 per-cent, as against 4 per-cent yielded by India stock, not only enhanced its value to the native holder, but also proved that the English themselves had full confidence in the stability of the Indian Government, and were quite ready to back their opinion with their money—a fact which the natives had been much inclined to doubt; and from that time onward the Indian capitalist lent much more freely than ever he had done before. "Enfaced" rupee paper—the portion, that is to say, which is held in Europe—amounts, at the present time, to about a third of the whole issue, and is a favourite investment, or, rather, a favourite speculation with those who believe that silver still has a future before it. The

---

* "Enfacement" is the antonym of *endorsement*, which obviously suggested it. This seems to be its first appearance in public, and it was, doubtless, coined for the occasion to express a form of words written, printed, or stamped on the face of a bill, note, or other document. Though a useful addition to the language, it has never come into general use, except in "enfaced rupee paper", and has escaped the notice of nearly every lexicographer.

comparative expediency of raising money in England or in India depends, now-a-days, on several considerations. The advantage of borrowing in India is two-fold. On political grounds it is advisable that the native should be encouraged to hold a stake in the country; and, on financial grounds, it is advisable both that the debt should be incurred in silver, the metal in which the revenue is received, and that the country should have the benefit of the fund-holder's expenditure. The disadvantages are, firstly, that on silver loans raised in India a higher rate of interest must be paid than on gold loans negotiated here; and, secondly, that there is difficulty in obtaining the amount required, and obtaining it quickly, as the Government has never yet succeeded in attracting the petty savings of the people, who prefer either to lay out their money in ornaments, or to employ it in usury. To borrowing in the London market, where money is abundant and cheap, the one great drawback is, that the interest must be met in gold, and that the Government hazards a serious loss in converting its silver. Thus, if India borrows £1,000 here at 2¼ per-cent when the exchange is at 1s. 3d., she receives Rs.1,600, and has to pay £25 interest, which is provided by selling a council draft for 400 rupees. If the exchange now rises to 1s. 4d., the £25 interest will cost her only 375 rupees; but if, on the contrary, it were to fall to, say 1s., the interest would amount to 500 rupees. The point to be determined, therefore, is whether the difference of interest does, or does not, counterbalance the risk of loss in exchange. In other words, if the Indian Government can borrow 25 per-cent cheaper in London than it can in Calcutta—that is to say, at 2¼ per-cent as against 3¼ per-cent—is 25 per-cent a sufficient premium to cover the risk of a future fall in silver? Taking the rupee at the conventional rate of two shillings, the total debt of India amounted, on 31 March 1896, to—

In England	£115,903,732
In India ...	103,188,928

and is, therefore, pretty equally divided between internal and external loans. A peculiar feature in connection with the external debt is, that India has to obtain the permission of Parliament before issuing a loan here. No other Government has to do so. Our self-governing colonies are at full liberty to borrow as much as they please in London on their own responsibility, and so are all foreign States. If the king of Patagonia, for example, likes to go to the expense of printing and advertising a prospectus, he may publicly invite subscriptions to his 10 per-cent Government Loan of five millions at 60, and need ask leave of no one. But if the Secretary of State for India wants to buy a railway with English capital, he has first to convince Parliament that the proposed outlay is legitimate and necessary, and is not allowed to raise the money until an Act has been passed authorizing him to do so. The origin of the practice is curious. The East India Company, in its first beginnings, was a chartered association of adventurers, possessing certain exclusive privileges of trade (like the African companies of to-day), and it was only by accident that, in course of time, it acquired its sovereign governing authority. Being no more, at the outset, than a simple trading company, its borrowing powers were limited by Parliament, just as at the present time the borrowing powers of railway companies are limited. When it eventually developed into a great political body, and dropped its mercantile functions, the directors took the opinion of counsel as to whether there was any legal obstacle to their contracting funded debt in this country, and were advised that there existed no hindrance to their so doing; but when, in 1858, it was found necessary to resort to the London market for assistance, and the directors contemplated testing their right, the Government thought, and represented to them, that, inasmuch as it had been the invariable practice for Parliament to authorize them to borrow on bonds in this country, it would not be expedient to act on the opinion expressed by counsel, and that it would be more respectful to Parliament to apply for express permission, as had always been done before. Application was, therefore, made in the usual way, and an Act was passed (21 Vict., c. III), the preamble of which recites that, " In consequence of the disturbances in India, it is expedient " that the East India Company should be enabled to raise " money in the United Kingdom on the credit of the revenues " of India." This was in March 1858, and before six months were over, the East India Company—the most famous joint-stock association of which there is any record—had ceased to exist; but the course taken by it in asking for power to enable it to borrow here, was regarded as a precedent by the new India Council, which took over all the company's responsibilities, and when, in the following year, more money was required, the same step was again taken of requesting Parliament to sanction the loan. Another Act (22 Vict., c. XI) was accordingly passed, which, *mutatis mutandis*, was almost a copy of the statute of the previous year, and which stated in the preamble that, " In consequence of the recent disturb-" ances in India, it is expedient that *the Secretary of State in* " *Council of India* should be enabled to raise money in the " United Kingdom on the credit of the revenues of India" ; and from that day to this the same practice of asking leave to borrow has been invariably pursued. There is one other topic to be considered before we leave the subject of the Debt of India, and that is the question whether England, in authorizing India to borrow, virtually assumes the responsibility of seeing that India's creditors shall be paid in full, and thus creates a contingent charge on her own revenue. No one supposes that any legal liability rests on the Imperial Exchequer. On that point the law is as plain and clear as it well can be. Every India Loan Bill contains a clause enacting that the principal and interest thereby secured " shall be " charged on, and payable out of, the revenues of India, in " like manner as other liabilities incurred on account of the " government of the said territories " ; and there is no word that can be construed into a guarantee on the part of this country. It was, in fact, with a view to completely settle all controversy that the Government first introduced that clause in 1858, and, so far as the contract is concerned, the terms are too distinct to admit of any doubt that the holder of Indian funds lends his money on the security of the Indian revenue, and on that security alone. It is not on the ground of right, however, that doubts arise, but on the ground of policy. Having assumed the responsibility of governing India, can we dissociate from that responsibility the obligation of meeting the engagements chargeable on Indian revenue ? Looking at the fact that upwards of a hundred millions have been lent to India by European capitalists, would it be morally possible for this country to altogether repudiate the Indian Debt without seriously endangering its own credit ? This is a question which—as Lord Stanley said, in 1859, in words that to-day, in presence of the ominous aspect of the silver problem, have a prophetic sound—" will recur again and " again, and which will have to be considered *in the future* as " well as in the present." Many other eminent men have also questioned the feasibility of our being able to answer that we "decline to intervene" if ever the creditor of India should have to present his protested bill to us, "in case of need." " Depend upon it", said Sir Robert Peel, when Prime Minister, in 1842, "if the credit of India should become disordered, if " some great exertion should become necessary, then the credit " of England must be brought forward to its support." Again, "It is idle", said Mr. Disraeli, when Chancellor of the Exchequer, in 1858, "any longer to distinguish between " Indian and English finance. If the President of the India " Council—a Queen's Minister in Downing Street—should " find it necessary to raise money by public loan to pay " Her Majesty's troops in India, it will be idle, when the " dividends are due on that loan, to pretend to assert that he " will be able to say, if the means are not at hand, the " exchequer of India is empty, and the revenue of India is " alone liable." I might cite further instances, but these will suffice to show that, notwithstanding the absence of a specific guarantee, many of our leading statesmen have been of opinion that a refusal to help India in case of emergency, would neither be generous nor wise. Moreover, there are good grounds for asserting that it would not even be practicable. The fund-holder's charge on Indian revenue is a first charge, which he can enforce, if necessary, by suing the Secretary for India, and if, after paying him, the revenue proved insufficient to meet the cost of the civil and military establishments, we should either have to maintain the Governor-General and the army at our own expense, or leave India without administration and without defence. On the other side of the question it has been argued, that if we were once to admit responsibility in the case of India, we should have to apply the same rule to Canada and Australia, which also raise money on the security of their own revenues. But the cases are quite dissimilar. The colonies govern themselves; they have representative institutions; they determine upon their own policy, contract their own debts, and impose their own taxes. India, on the other hand, is under a regulated despotism, and its people have no voice, either in their government or in their taxation. Besides which, colonial debt has been contracted for colonial purposes only, while a great part of the expenditure charged against India has been incurred in fighting to maintain our supremacy. On this question of guarantee, there appeared in the *Times*, last August, a letter from Mr. Benjamin Cohen, a well-known authority on finance, which states the matter so well that I think I will read it to you. He says: " I suggest once more, as I did in the House of Commons in " 1895, that the money raised by loan by the Indian Govern- " ment should be raised, in future, with the Imperial guarantee. " It is true such a step as I advocate would not secure for the " Indian Government, now, anything like the saving that " would have resulted had it been taken in former years. " The credit of the Indian Government is now, and deserves " to be, almost as good as that of the home Government. " But that, surely, is an argument in favour of, and not against, " my proposal, while it is certain that there never has been a " moment when such a policy would have more political " effect on the loyal population of India, as well as on the " insignificant, but still not to be ignored, disloyal portion of " the native population. While, therefore, it appears to me " there is everything to be gained by such a guarantee " being given, and given specially at this moment, there is " absolutely nothing to be lost. The relations between the " home and the Indian Governments are different from those " subsisting between the executive Government at home and " any other part of Her Majesty's dominions. India is not a " self-governing nor a Crown colony. All her finance, all her " fiscal arrangements are subject to the approval of the " Secretary of State in Council. She can neither take off nor " impose a single tax, nor raise a rupee by loan, without the " sanction of the Government at home. She would be " responsible, as now, for every penny raised, and would be " able, as now, to meet her engagements. Of this, I suppose, " no one has any doubt, and certainly none is entertained in " the City, as is shown by the level at which her credit " stands", &c. One proposal made at the time when the subject was under discussion, was, that India should borrow from the home Government, paying just the same rate as she would have had to give in the open market, and that the home Government should apply the difference of 1 per-cent between the rate paid for the money by India, and the rate at which she herself could borrow, to a sinking fund, which, in fifty years, or less, would extinguish the debt. To this excellent suggestion the chief objection appears to have been that it might encourage India to be extravagant, and that she would never exert herself to pay her own way, unless we gave her clearly to understand that she must depend on herself alone. I think the objection very weak indeed, and it is a great pity that the idea was never carried out, as the sinking fund, by this time, would have wiped out a great portion of the debt. The final outcome of the controversy was, that a middle course was adopted. While positively refusing to admit the principle that this country could, in any event, be held answerable for the debts contracted by our protégé, Parliament, at the same time, came to the conclusion that it would be well, for the future, to keep a more watchful eye over Indian finance; and, since 1858, it has not only subjected Indian expenditure to close scrutiny, and taken care that no unnecessary charge should be imposed on Indian revenue, but has also insisted on full explanations being given whenever it has been proposed to increase the external debt. So far we have been discussing the position of the bond-holder in case of India's insolvency. What his position might be, in the very improbable event of our giving up India, or, in the still more improbable event of our being driven out of India, are cases that fall outside the range of practical possibilities, and which it would be unprofitable to waste time over.

Our examination of the stocks forming the first group in the official List is now at an end, and as it would be inexpedient, at this advanced stage, to broach the subject of Corporation Stocks, which stand next in order for consideration, I purpose directing your attention, in the few minutes that remain at our disposal, to the subject of Trust Investments. When Mr. Goschen introduced his conversion scheme in 1888, it was represented to the Government that the reduction of interest would operate very harshly in the case of stock held by trustees, the interest derived from which was, in many instances, all that widows and orphans had to depend upon, and that to suddenly deprive a helpless class of people, who usually have no means of earning a livelihood, of a part of their small fixed incomes for the benefit of the taxpayer, would be to inflict upon them a grave injustice. As there was really no reason, it was also said, why the beneficiary of a trust should not be allowed as full an enjoyment of the produce of the fund as was consistent with the safety of the capital—this latter being always the paramount consideration —it was suggested, as a remedy, that the limited range of investment, to which the trustee's choice had hitherto been restricted by law, should be extended, in order to include such other securities as would, while equally safe, yield a somewhat better return. Though Mr. Goschen did not appear to like the proposal—seeming to consider it desirable that trust-money should be employed to support the credit of the State— he, nevertheless, promised to think the matter over, and in the following year a Trust Investment Act was passed, which, in addition to consolidating the existing law on the subject, gave trustees much wider powers of selection than they had up to that time possessed. Until that Bill became law, the securities in which trustees might invest—failing express directions in the trust deed—were only to be ascertained by searching through a number of Acts. The first of these, passed in 1859 (before which year the trustee might have incurred personal liability if he had purchased anything but consols or other Government securities), authorized investment in Bank Stock and East India Stock; in 1867, the authority was extended to any stock, the interest on which was guaranteed by Parliament; in 1871, to Metropolitan Consols; and in 1882, to first-class railway debenture stocks. The necessity for all this piecemeal legislation was of a two-fold nature ; on the one hand there had been an enormous increase in the amount of trust funds, which were growing, as proved by the yield of the death duties, at the rate of millions a year, and which are believed to amount, at the present time, to something like £200,000,000, and on the other, there was a concurrent decrease in the available supply of Government securities, which were being steadily absorbed, both by the operation of the sinking fund, and by the purchases of the Court of Chancery and of the Savings' Bank authorities. The policy pursued by Parliament with regard to the successive additions to the authorized list, had been to select only from among such securities as were subject to the jurisdiction of the British courts, and also, as far as possible, from these over which it might be said to exercise control to the extent of determining to what amount they should be issued; and this, you will find, was the guiding principle that was also followed in drawing up the Trust Investment Act of 1889.

LONDON DAILY STOCK AND SHARE LIST.

FIFTH LECTURE.

[Delivered 21 February 1898.]

YOU will remember that, when discussing the obligations
which represent our indebtedness as a nation, I had occasion
to point out, as a matter of congratulation, that, in com-
pliance with the general wish of all political parties, and
thanks to our enjoyment of a prolonged period of peace
and prosperity, continuous efforts had been made for many
years past to lighten the pressure of our huge incumbrance,
and had been attended with so great a measure of success
that, from its highest point of £900,000,000, which the
National Debt attained at the close of the great war, the total
had now shrunk to less than £650,000,000. So far as it goes,
this is, of course, eminently satisfactory; but a glance at the
next item in the Official List, that of Corporation Stocks, is
calculated to arouse some misgiving as to whether a bald
statement that the Public Debt has been reduced by upwards of
£250,000,000 conveys the whole of the truth; and, on turning to
the Local Taxation Returns, our doubts are confirmed, for we
are there brought face to face with the unpleasant and, at first
sight, startling fact that the diminution of one description of
national indebtedness has been accompanied by the creation
and growth of another, and that practically the whole of the
money so laboriously scraped together by the Imperial
authority for the benefit of its creditors has been re-borrowed

by our local authorities, who, at the end of March 1895—the date of the latest available return—had piled up a liability amounting to no less than £235,000,000. The first year for which the Local Taxation Returns give the amount of the Local Debt is 1874–75.

In that year it is stated to have been	£92,820,100
And the National Debt was ...	755,619,537
	£848,439,637

In 1880–81 the respective figures were:

Local Debt	£144,203,299
National Debt ...	734,670,016
	£878,873,315

And in 1894–95:

Local Debt	£235,335,049
National Debt	656,998,941
	£892,333,990

The decrease of the one has, therefore, in the last twenty years, been more than counterbalanced by the increase of the other. Taking the two classes of indebtedness together, moreover, our national obligations, at the present time, are almost as onerous as ever they were. It may be objected, however, with some sort of plausibility, that this presentment of the case brings into conjunction, and places an unfair construction upon, facts which are entirely disconnected, and that no useful purpose can be served by linking the National with the Local Debt, inasmuch as the two are of essentially different natures. The National Debt, it is commonly said, is the heritage of costly and mostly useless wars; and all that we have to show for it—apart from warships, telegraph lines, government buildings, and the Suez Canal shares—is an indefinite amount of prestige and glory. The Local Debt, on the other hand, has been incurred in providing for the requirements of a higher civilization, and for a great portion of it we are able to point to tangible and realizable assets, in the shape of valuable, and in many instances reproductive, property, acquired and held for the enjoyment of the public for ever. If full justice is to be done to the subject of Corporation Stocks, which we are about to enter upon, it will be necessary to discuss the growth and

development of this Local Debt in some detail, as well as to ask
whether the expenditure of so large a sum of borrowed money
has been justified by the benefits received from it, and whether
local indebtedness has now reached its approximate limit, or is
likely to continue growing until it finally becomes as great as,
or even greater than, the National Debt itself. To discover
the beginnings of Local Debt, we must go back as far as 1792,
in which year the system originated of advancing public money
to local bodies in furtherance of objects approved of by
Parliament. The usual purpose for which assistance was
given was the carrying on of relief works for the alleviation of
distress; but, in some instances, loans were also granted
for the promotion of important public works, such as land
drainage, river embankments, &c., the execution of which,
though of acknowledged necessity, did not fall within the
scope of Government operations. It is unnecessary to go
further into the history of these State loans, as we went over
the same ground in connection with the subject of Local Loans
Stock; but I may mention that the practice of borrowing from
Government—though now chiefly confined to small communities
who require sums too trivial to be worth asking for in
the open market—still exists, and has been extended to
numerous objects. For upwards of half-a-century the growth
of the debt was a matter of insignificance, and it is only
when we come to the present reign, and to the new era of
reformed corporations, inaugurated by the Municipal Reform
Act of 1835, that it begins to assume importance. Up to that time
the privilege of incorporation had been either granted to serve
political ends or acquired by purchase, and as it so happened
that the governing councils nominated by most of the early
charters were given the right to appoint their own successors,
there had gradually grown up in our great towns exclusive
and independent corporations, which had succeeded in
monopolizing privileges belonging to the borough as a whole,
and had in many cases even assumed to themselves the sole right
of returning members to Parliament. Owing to the notorious
jobbery and corruption to which this system gave rise, the
inhabitants of incorporated towns had long manifested a
general and just dissatisfaction with their municipal institutions, and one of the first duties of the reformed Parliament of
1832, was the appointment of a Commission to enquire into
the constitution and privileges of civic corporations. The

Commissioners discovered disgraceful abuses, and reported that "the existing municipal corporations of England and Wales "neither possess nor deserve public confidence or respect, and "that a thorough reform must be effected before they can "become, what they ought to be, useful and efficient instruments "of local government." The outcome of their recommendations was the great charter of English municipal liberties, the Municipal Corporations Act of 1835, which enlarged the basis of local representation, put an end to the abuses exposed by the Commissioners, and provided a uniform constitution for all boroughs to which it applied. It also provided for the creation by charter of new municipalities. If the inhabitants of an unincorporated town deem themselves worthy of the dignity of a mayor and corporation, they may petition for a charter, which on their convincing the Privy Council of their fitness to be entrusted with the privilege, will be granted them, unless good cause appears for withholding it. What we call a town, it may be well to explain, has no legal existence as such, and its name is no more than a geographical expression, identifying a certain collection of houses larger than a village. The law may recognize a parish, or a sanitary district of that name, but knows not the town until it is incorporated, and has been scheduled as one of the boroughs to which the Act applies. Its government thereafter rests in the hands of a local representative body, the Town Council, and, as a municipal corporation, it becomes endowed with a perpetual succession —that is to say, however the members may fluctuate, the corporate body never ceases to exist—and with the power of holding lands in mortmain. The Act of 1835 was amended by numerous subsequent enactments, and was eventually superseded by "The Municipal Corporations Act, 1882", which consolidated the whole of the law on the subject.

The success that attended the first great experiment in local self-government, as manifested in the growth of a municipal administration far more vigorous and intelligent than had been possible during the era of close corporations, speedily led to a great extension in the powers conferred upon towns of managing their own affairs; and the legislation of the last fifty years has cast upon local authorities a constant succession of new duties and new responsibilities. In the attempt to cope with the multiform and ever-increasing wants of society, their labours have grown with the growth of their capacity; and were it but generally realized how greatly the internal welfare of the community,—its health, and its safety, its pleasures and its comforts,—depends on the wisdom and foresight displayed by our local administrators, the subject of local administration would surely meet with the attention it deserves. To them is confided the relief of the distressed poor, the maintenance of elementary schools, the control of the police, and the management of numerous endowments. They provide baths and wash-houses for the poor, hospitals for the sick, workhouses for the destitute, asylums for the lunatic, and graves for all. Under one group of Acts, they cleanse, drain, repair and light our streets. Another bids them erect healthy dwellings for the poor, and keep an eye on common lodging-houses. We look to them to regulate the traffic, to give us libraries and public parks, and even to see that the so-called comic song of the music-hall pays due regard to the conventionalities of public decorum. They register our coming into the world, and, if necessary, vaccinate and educate us; they record our departure from it, and, if need be, bury us. Of all their functions, the most important, however, is the care of the public health. The present reign witnessed the first serious attempts that have ever been made to solve the hygienic problems that spring from the crowding together in great towns of dense masses of human beings, and systematic sanitary legislation may be said to begin with the Public Health Act of 1848. Water supply, food analysis, the main-tenance of sewers and drains, measures to arrest the spread of infection, the inspection and prevention of nuisances, and such like, have been the chief subjects of this legislation, which has necessarily applied more to towns than to the country. The dweller in rural districts still sinks his own well and digs his own cesspool, but in towns the householder is absolutely dependent on the cistern and the dust-cart. Another Public Health Act came into force in 1875. It effected little actual change, however, in the existing sanitary law, but, by codifying the large number of statutes relating to it, rendered it simpler and more intelligible. The long catalogue of offices under-taken by local authorities is even yet not exhausted. Provincial municipalities have shown an increasing disposition, for many years past, to supplant private enterprise by joint action in the supply of such public conveniences or necessities as are of the nature of monopolies, and by including the sale of gas and water, and of cemetery lots, within the sphere of their activity, have been able to apply a considerable margin of profit towards the relief of local rates. Latterly, too, they have been turning their attention to electric lighting, and to the acquisition of tramways, while one great corporation—that of Manchester—has been investing money in a ship canal, and talks now of establishing a municipal theatre. It is not to be supposed, of course, that duties so numerous and so varied can all be performed by one class of authority. Nor is such the case. In addition to County Councils, District Councils and Parish Councils, to Boards of Guardians and Boards of Health, we find Local Boards, School Boards, Highway Boards, Burial Boards, Harbour Boards, Vestries, Commissioners, and a dozen others. But if the ratepayer attempts to discover which is which of these bodies, to trace out their relations to each other, to distinguish between their functions, to map out their administrative areas, and, in short, to find out for himself how, and by whom, he is rated and governed, the complexity of the subject will strike terror to his soul. It would almost appear that, whenever it has become necessary to legislate for a new social want, Parliament has made provision for it, quite regardless of existing machinery and existing areas. We have parishes and unions; we have urban and rural sanitary districts; we have school board areas, highway districts, and what not; almost all independent of each other, and, as often as not, interlacing and overlapping. "For almost every new " administrative function the Legislature has provided a new " area containing a new constituency, who, by a new method of " election, choose candidates who satisfy a new qualification, to " sit upon a new board, during a new term, to levy a new rate, " and to spend a good deal of the new revenues in paying new " officers, and erecting new buildings. Thus there has been " created, not a system, but a chaos; a chaos of areas, a chaos of " elections, a chaos of authorities, a chaos of rates, a chaos of " returns." The consequence is, that not one householder in a thousand understands the construction and working of the machinery of local government; in fact, the great majority of us scarcely know even as much as the names of the motley crowd of public authorities by whom the local business of the district is carried on, and by whom our money is spent. The system defies criticism, simply because so few of us can spare the time and trouble to find out what it is and what it does.

F

All we know for certain is, that the rates grow heavier year by year, and that they must be paid; and we pay and grumble.

To all who have paid the least attention to matters of finance, it is perfectly well known that the cost of public works of any magnitude is rarely, if ever, defrayed out of current revenue. In the first place, it is obvious that, if a work is of permanent utility, it would be most unfair to make those who happen to be residing in the district at the time of its construction pay for that which will last long after they may have removed or died. Then, again, when it has been once decided that certain work must be done—a main sewer constructed, or a town hall built—it is best that the work should proceed quickly, and without interruption. It would be quite possible, of course, to build gradually, spending as much each year as the ordinary revenue allowed, and then suspending operations until additional funds accumulated; but, in most cases, the certain consequence of delay would be damage to the work already done, and it is the common experience in such matters that waste of time is waste of money. Generally speaking, therefore, it is essential, before beginning any important undertaking, that there should be sufficient money at command to ensure its completion, and the principle is, nowadays, firmly established of borrowing the requisite capital, and of spreading the repayment of principal and interest over a term of years. Now, a corporation or other local authority cannot, any more than an individual, borrow a large sum of money without giving security for its repayment; and it cannot give security—that is to say, it cannot legally pledge the rates—without express statutory authority. Being a creation of the law, it is possessed only of such rights and privileges as the law bestows upon it. Until 1848, however, the facilities which are now so common for deferring to a future day the greater part of the payment for local improvements had only been granted by Parliament in some exceptional cases, where special application had been made; and, as a consequence, our towns had shown themselves extremely unwilling to lay out money on such unremunerative objects as drainage, sewerage, and paving, because the ratepayers objected to being saddled with the whole of the cost. As this neglect of sanitary measures was costing the country thousands of lives each year, and undermining the health of the whole urban population, it became necessary to overcome their reluctance by removing its cause, and in the Public Health Act of that year, which enforced a heavy expenditure, Parliament not only authorized all local authorities administering the statute to levy a new rate for improvements, but also empowered them to raise capital by mortgaging the said rate, and to pay back by instalments. The snow-ball of local debt was thus fairly set rolling; and before many years had passed, its growth was fostered and encouraged by a variety of subsequent acts, which aimed at improving the social condition and general health of the people, and which invariably conferred fresh powers of borrowing. At the outset, and for a long time afterwards, almost all these loans were obtained from the State, through the medium of the Public Works Loan Commissioners, but the great inconvenience which this system occasioned to the Treasury, from the fact of frequently having to honour large drafts when funds were low and money dear, led the Government, in 1875, to introduce a Local Loans Act, with a view to encourage local authorities to go to the open market for what they wanted. To some extent they had already done so, having borrowed considerable sums by private arrangement, from solicitors and insurance companies, &c., as they still do, but the security which they were able to offer—that of a mortgage deed, charging a specified rate—besides being inconvenient and expensive, was not readily negotiable, and appealed only to a special and limited class of investor. Thinking that facilities for issuing a a more marketable form of security might induce the municipalities to try their luck in the money market, instead of coming with a petition to Downing Street, the Government gave them liberty, by means of the Local Loans Act, to create debentures, debenture stock, or annuity certificates; and, in order to tempt the appetite of the ordinary investor, made provision for the official sanction of their loans by the Local Government Board, such sanction to be conclusive evidence that the borrower had power to issue the security, and that the same was in conformity with the Act, thus rendering it indisputable. Though the Act was a distinct step in advance, inasmuch as it clearly recognized the principle that the form given to an acknowledgment of debt is an important element in the success of its issue, yet it met with very little favour, and is practically a dead letter. The mistake made was that of requiring that the debenture, or debenture stock, should be a specific charge on a particular local rate or property, a condition, the result of which would be to split up the debt of a town into a number of small divisions—one issue of stock being secured, let us say, on the district rate, and another on the poor rate; one batch of debentures charged on the markets, another on the gas works, another on the town hall, and so forth. But as the marketability of a security depends on its quantity as well as on its quality, that is to say, on the fact of its existing in sufficient bulk to render buying or selling easy within narrow limits, the effect of sub-division is to detract from its value; and this objection proved fatal. Besides which, the corporations had other ideas. The phenomenal success of a daring experiment attempted a year or two previously by the Metropolitan Board of Works, had set them thinking of a new departure in their system of finance. Formerly, the Board of Works had raised money, like other borrowers, by the cumbrous method of mortgaging the rates; but, having exhausted its credit in that direction, it had obtained permission in 1869 to make a direct appeal to capitalists by the issue of a Consolidated Three-and-a-Half per-cent Stock, the service of which was made a first charge on the whole of its property and revenues. The advantage of this plan was that, in lieu of renewable mortgages at various rates of interest, differing in priority and charged upon different securities, the entire debt became merged into one homogeneous class of obligation, which was simple, uniform, and intelligible in all its conditions, and which was secured on the whole body of the assets without distinction. Though a stock based upon rates, instead of on taxes, was a distinct novelty to investors, it had grown greatly in favour since its attributes came to be better understood—so much so, indeed, that an issue of £2,600,000 offered in 1874 at 94½ had been subscribed for eight times over, and, before the Local Loans Bill became law, the stock had risen to 102. It needed little insight on the part of the local authorities to discover that the true solution of the problem "how to borrow cheaply, quickly, and conveniently", had now been found, and, turning their backs on the facilities placed at their disposal by the Local Loans Act, they were soon busily at work drafting private Bills, which should bestow also upon them the coveted right and privilege of issuing the new-fashioned Corporation Stock.

The borrowing powers of corporations are derived either

from the general law, or from private Bills. Under the former they may borrow with the sanction of a Government Department, in virtue of the authority conferred by the Public Health Acts, the Elementary Education Act, the Artisans' Dwellings Act, and numerous others, for the purposes authorized by the respective statutes; but, under the latter, they may borrow for any purpose that Parliament can be induced to approve of. Under the former, again, they may borrow either from the State or from the public; under the latter, from the public only. When borrowing from the public under the general law they had formerly to choose between issuing a mortgage-deed, or adopting one of the methods authorized by the Local Loans Act; but in private Bills they almost invariably asked for authority to issue Corporation Stock. Until quite recently the power to create Stock, other than Debenture Stock, could only be obtained by a special Act, and, as the expense of promoting a private Bill is very considerable, the smaller corporations were practically debarred from issuing it. In 1890, however, an Act was passed—"The Public Health Acts Amendment Act" —which authorizes its creation by all urban sanitary authorities. The enabling clause, s. 52, is as follows: "Where any "authority, whether a municipal corporation, local board, or "improvement commissioners, which is an urban authority, have "for the time being, either in their capacity as urban authority, "or in any other capacity, any power to borrow money, they "may, with the consent of the Local Government Board, exercise "such power by the creation of stock, to be created, issued, "transferred, dealt with, and redeemed in such manner, and in "accordance with such regulations as the Local Government "Board may from time to time prescribe." This Act has been very freely taken advantage of, and, since 1890, many small towns have been able to borrow by issuing stock at 3 per-cent, while if they had applied to the Public Works Loan Commissioners they would probably have had to pay $3\frac{1}{2}$ per-cent for the money. Such control as is exercised over the borrowing powers of Corporations rests almost entirely in the hands of the Local Government Board. This Board, the duties of which extend far and wide, and which is the mainspring of the sanitary organization of the country, was established in 1871, with the object of concentrating in one department of the Government the supervision, which till then had been shared between the Home Secretary, the Privy Council, and the Board of Trade, of the laws relating to the public health, to the relief of the poor, and to local government. No loan can be raised by a sanitary authority under the general law without its express sanction, which is only given after enquiry to show that the money is required for a proper purpose, that the works proposed are sufficient for their object, and will, without doubt, last good for at least as long a time as that limited for the repayment of the loan, and that the estimates, of which full details must be supplied, are fair and reasonable. This enquiry is held in the district concerned by one of the Local Board inspectors, and public notice is given of it, in order that the ratepayers and other persons interested may have the opportunity of expressing any objection they may entertain to the scheme. If land should be required for the proposed works, the purchase of which is hindered by the caprice of its owners, the Board may also grant a Provisional Order for its compulsory acquisition; but the Order only becomes operative after its confirmation by Parliament. In the case of private Acts that comprise borrowing powers, a copy of the Bill must be lodged with the Board, which reports upon it to the Select Committee of the House appointed to hear the evidence on the subject. Its recommendations always have great weight, even if they are not invariably adopted. Borrowers under private Acts are also required to furnish the Board with annual returns showing the exact position of their loan accounts. It is hardly necessary to say that local Acts never confer unlimited borrowing powers. The corporation must specify the amount it requires and prove its estimates before the committee. As already mentioned, it is an axiom with the Local Government Board that the time allowed for the repayment of a loan should be regulated by the probable duration of the work to be constructed, so that the burden of the expenditure may be borne by the generation that chiefly benefits by it; but, with regard to private Bills, Parliament appears, for many years, to have observed no fixed principle in its practice, and cases were not uncommon in which local authorities were allowed as much as a full century in which to pay back the money borrowed for gas and water works. There can be little doubt, in fact, that the expectation of obtaining a longer term for the repayment of their loans under private Bills than would have been permitted them under the general law, operated as a strong inducement to some of the local authorities to include in their local Acts powers of borrowing for the execution of works which ought, in strictness, to have been carried out under public Acts, and that the laxity displayed by Parliament in this respect led to much money being spent on objects which might very well have waited a few years longer. It will hardly be disputed that the ease with which the Governments of civilized and semi-civilized States have been able during the past thirty or forty years to contract permanent, or quasi-permanent, debt, and to bequeath to posterity the fetters forged by their folly, or their misfortune, has been a fatal facility, and in too many instances has proved to be an abiding curse. There is all the more reason, therefore, why, with this experience before us, our local authorities should be restrained from drawing at too long a date on the ratepayer of the future. That unfortunate individual will have quite enough to do to provide for his own wants and require-ments, without having to repay money in the expenditure of which he had no voice, and which, for any benefit that he may derive from it, need very likely never have been spent at all. Besides, the very fact of being able to incur debts for others to settle opens the door to extravagance and jobbery. With borrowing rendered so easy that it is but to ask and have, and repayment so easy that the money will scarcely be missed, it is hardly to be wondered at that local authorities should shrink from the hard and thankless task of opposing expenditure on betterments and embellishments which, whether justifiable or not, are always popular and plausible. That "Borrowing dulls the edge of husbandry" is as true now as in the days of Polonius. Then, again, to have the handling and disposal of these enormous sums means the wielding of great power and influence, and, in more ways than one, must be a very agree-able thing; so that it would be irrational to suppose that Town Councils will ever be found over-jealous in their advocacy of a wise and prudent economy. One hundred years is, in fact, much too long a time to keep open any municipal liability, and, for all practical purposes, is little better than no term of repayment at all. Even in the case of water works, which are perhaps the most durable of the purposes for which long loans have been granted, it is doubtful whether they can be con-structed to last for a century without extensive and costly repairs; while as to gas works it is obvious, in view of the growing competition of the electric light, that the cost ought to be written off at a far more rapid rate. In 1882, the attention of Parliament was directed to the urgent need of checking this great evil, and the House of Commons determined, by a new Standing Order (No. 173a), that the extreme limit for the repayment of loans to be henceforth authorized by local Acts should be sixty years. For the future, therefore, fresh borrowing powers for a longer period than sixty years can only be given by the suspension of the Standing Order, which ran as follows: "In the case of any Bill promoted by "or conferring powers on a Municipal Corporation or Local "Board, Improvement Commissioners, or other local authority, "the Committee on the Bill are to consider the clauses of the "Bill with reference to the following matters: *(a)* Whether "the Bill gives powers relating to police or sanitary regulations "in conflict with, deviation from, or excess of the provisions or "powers of the general law. *(b)* Whether the Bill gives "powers which may be obtained by means of bye-laws made "subject to the restrictions of general Acts already existing. "*(c)* Whether the Bill assigns a period for repayment of any "loans under the Bill exceeding the term of sixty years, which "term the Committee are not in any case to allow to be "exceeded, or any period disproportionate to the duration of "the works to be executed, or other objects of the loan. "*(d)* Whether the Bill gives borrowing powers for purposes "for which such powers already exist, or may be obtained "under general Acts without subjecting the exercise of the "powers under the Bill to approval from time to time by the "proper Government Department. The Committee are to "report specially to the House in what manner any clauses "relating to the several matters aforesaid have been dealt with "by them; and whether any Report from any Government "Department relative to the Bill has been referred to the "Committee; and, if so, in what manner the recommendations "in that Report have been dealt with by the Committee, and "any other circumstances of which, in the opinion of the "Committee, it is desirable that the House should be informed; "and the Report of the Committee is to be printed and "circulated with the Votes." Sixty years, it may be mentioned, is the period fixed by the Metropolitan Board of Works Loan Acts, as well as for loans under the Public Health Act. The term cannot be regarded as a hardship by corporations, seeing that it only entails an annual sinking fund of ⅜ per-cent (invested at 3 per-cent) to pay off the debt.

Notwithstanding the fact that the considerations advanced by those who oppose the creation of long-term local debts have gained acceptance to the extent of influencing legislation, it would be a mistake to infer that nothing remains to be said on the other side of the question. It has been maintained, for instance, that, though it may be right to insist on the early repayment of debts created for local improvements or other unremunerative purposes, the reasoning that leads to this conclusion does not apply with equal force to loans raised for the acquisition of water works, tramways, &c., which stand on an entirely different footing. Outlay of this description being essentially an investment of municipal capital in co-operative business enterprise, it is held that the treatment of the capital account ought to be governed by the usual commercial principles that would obtain in the case of a well-managed joint-stock concern of similar nature. The capital of an ordinary water or tramway company is represented by the plant in which it has been invested, and, so long as the original good order and condition are strictly kept up out of revenue, it is not expected that the cost of the property should be systematically redeemed, though it is, of course, wise to set up a reserve fund as provision against contingencies. Without going so far as to assert that a corporation should be allowed to issue perpetual stock against its investments in trading undertakings, it has been submitted that these grounds justify much longer terms of repayment than are now usually granted. That is not the only argument, however. At the present time another and far more serious contention is being urged, which threatens to become one of the burning questions of the day. It is contended, namely, that the incidence of local taxation is grossly unfair, and that, until it has been re-adjusted on a proper basis, the ratepayer ought not to be burdened with heavier repayments than are absolutely necessary. By local taxation is meant the charges levied on defined localities for supposed local purposes. Its principle is that the cost of such matters as concern only the dwellers in a particular neighbourhood, and not the nation at large, ought to be borne by the district affected; and the grievances to which it has given rise are that personalty does not bear its share, that the division of rates between occupier and owner is unequal, and that ground rents almost escape. It originates with the poor rate imposed on occupiers in the reign of Queen Elizabeth, at which time, and for long afterwards, the number of occupying owners was very large. The property of these occupying owners was the natural and obvious quarry of local levies; but owing to the comparative rarity of the tenant farmer class, the question of a division of the rate between owner, as such, and occupier, as such, was not raised, or if raised was disregarded. At first, relief of destitution was almost the only purpose for which a charge was made on occupancy; but in course of time other imposts came to be levied on the same assessment, and still continued to be exacted from occupiers, though these, in the great majority of cases, had ceased to be owners, and were now tenants. How anomalous the incidence of local taxes has become strikes one forcibly on contrasting it with that of the national taxes. In both cases the true principle is that all classes should contribute in proportion to their means. To this end the Chancellor of the Exchequer spreads his net as widely as possible, and always makes at least the pretence of distributing his attentions equally over the community, taxing both directly and indirectly, and taking tribute as well from real as from personal property. But the whole burden of rates falls on a particular class. Personal property has nothing to fear from them; but the moment capital is invested in landed property it falls a victim, and, though there is no doubt that a large part of the local outgoings directly affects and benefits houses and land, it cannot be claimed that any gain is derived from the expenditure on such matters as poor relief or elementary education. Hence, owners of real property complain of the injustice to which they are subject, and call for contributions from personalty. Then there is also the great wrong that, when owner and occupier are different persons, the occupier, and not the owner, is taxed. Thus, if money is borrowed for, let us say, necessary sewage works, the whole cost of paying the interest and extinguishing the principal is thrown upon householders, who are thereby compelled to improve the estate of the ground landlord at their own expense. The theory is, of course, that the tax ultimately falls upon the owner, because, if it were not imposed, he would be able to charge a higher rent for his house. This may be doubted; but if it be true that the owner pays all the rates in the end, it is a pity he cannot see his way to pay them in the beginning, and thus end the dispute. Certain it is that the discontent resulting from the belief of occupiers that they are made to pay for the improvement of other people's property is growing every day, and that local bodies now hardly dare undertake many useful works, because they dread the indignation that will be aroused by an increase of the rates.

The favour with which investors were from the first inclined to look upon corporation stocks, and of which the absorption within the last twenty years of upwards of £100,000,000 is substantial proof, was confirmed and increased by their inclusion in the list of stocks authorized by the Trust Funds Act of 1889; for, as it was known that the select committee, to whom the Bill was referred, had made searching enquiry into the soundness of local loans, and had satisfied itself that the security they offered was practically unexceptionable, any little doubt that the public may have felt on that score was entirely removed. Unless expressly forbidden by the instrument creating the trust, a trustee may now lawfully invest " (m) In nominal or inscribed stock issued, " or to be issued, by the corporation of any municipal borough, " having, according to the returns of the last census prior to " the date of investment, a population exceeding fifty thousand, " or by any county council, under the authority of any Act of " Parliament or Provisional Order ;" and the permission has been widely taken advantage of. The clause calls for the remark that, as the stability of a corporation stock does not depend on counting heads, it is not very obvious why a taboo should have been placed on the loans issued by incorporated towns of less than fifty thousand inhabitants, unless on the principle that a line had to be drawn somewhere. Perhaps the most curious result of that exception is the fact that the stock issued last year by the Corporation of the City of London is not a trust stock, simply because the population of the City does not attain the requisite minimum. The security offered by a corporation stock is that of a charge on the rates, which the corporation has power to levy, and on the whole of the revenue arising from its lands, markets, gas works, &c., and all other property for the time being. In case of default, provision is made for the appointment by the Court of Chancery of a receiver, but it need hardly be said that no occasion to exert the power has yet arisen. The assets of the corporations are doubtless of enormous value (the City of Manchester, for instance, appraises its corporate property at upwards of £14,000,000), but the ultimate and real security

for the debt is the rateable value of property, and rates form
the mainstay of local finance. The total Poor Rate Valuation
of England and Wales is upwards of £160,000,000 and, if we
assume that property is on the average worth from sixteen to
twenty years' purchase of the assessment, it is obvious that the
repayment of the debt of £235,000,000 is assured beyond all
reasonable doubt. It must also be borne in mind, that, as rates
are not limited in amount, a town must become absolutely
bankrupt before the security fails. Good as rates may be,
however, they are not equal to taxes as a debt security. Only
death or emigration to a desert island will relieve the taxpayer
of his burden; but the ratepayer can always shake off part of his
load by removing to a less heavily rated district. The weak point
about rates is, therefore, that if their pressure becomes too
severe they inevitably tend to drive trade outside the municipal
boundary, thus reducing both the rateable value and the local
revenue. As high rates may thus prove to be the forerunners
of local decay, their relative amount is a most important element
in the prosperity of a borough, and is a point that should always
be taken into consideration by the investor in corporation stocks.
Another test of comparative value is the ratio which the
unproductive portion of the debt—that part which represents
money spent and not money invested—bears to the rateable
value. To institute a comparison between the rateable value
and the entire debt is of every little use, because a borough
which has borrowed up to four or five times the amount of its
assessment, may possess such lucrative assets as to be in a
sounder position than another, the debt of which, though less
than its rateable value, may be represented solely by
unremunerative expenditure. Money spent in pulling down
slums, building board schools, and laying out recreation
grounds is money that has been well spent, and which in due
season will return an ample yield in the shape of an increase
in the health, happiness and intelligence of the people; but
from the investor's point of view a mortgage on health and
happiness presents an unsubstantial aspect, and he is apt to
remember that the entire charge of a debt incurred for such
purposes falls solely on the rates. As yet the process of
discrimination between the stocks of different corporations can
hardly be said to have begun. All are still regarded as about
equally good, just as Colonial Stocks used to be not many
years ago. But there are signs that it may not be long

deferred, and when that time does come—when the investor does at last begin to pick and choose—those towns which have borrowed most largely for unproductive purposes (and especially such among them as may be dependent on the prosperity of one particular industry), are likely to receive a rude reminder that they have long been treading on dangerous ground.

SIXTH LECTURE.

[Delivered 7 March 1891.]

AT our last meeting I was endeavouring to impress upon your minds the magnitude of the proportions attained by our Local Debt, which, though contracted by urban and rural authorities, solely for what are supposed to be local purposes, constitutes just as much a charge upon the national prosperity as do the Imperial obligations. Two hundred and thirty-five millions would be a large sum to owe, even if we had no National Debt. It means that every child born in England and Wales begins life £7. 16s. 7d. behindhand. It is as large as the Public Debt of India, or as that of all the Australasian Colonies combined, and even exceeds the total of the Public Debts of Germany, Holland, Sweden, Norway and Denmark, all added together. And yet, serious as is the fact of our handicapping the rising generation with so large an additional liability, its rapid growth appears to give rise to very little uneasiness, and notwithstanding the persistent efforts of a few statisticians to direct public attention to it, is regarded with all but complete apathy, being neither followed nor understood. While Imperial finance and taxation seem to be everybody's business, local finance and taxation are nobody's. Let twopence be added to the Income Tax, and we are ready to wreck the Government; let it be added to the rates, and we submit with resignation, because conscious of our abject

ignorance and helplessness. Now, large figures such as these
cannot be made to yield their true meaning without a certain
amount of manipulation. Simply to know that so great a sum
has been spent is not enough; we must know how and why it
has been spent. We ought also to know which of the purposes
are remunerative, and which not, and, with regard to the
capital expenditure for non-productive purposes, must ask to
what extent it was justifiable. In the Local Taxation Returns
for the financial year 1894–95, the outstanding debt in respect
of reproductive outlay, so far as it is practicable to identify it,
is stated to be as follows :

Water Works	£43,970,490
Gas Works ...	16,931,943
Markets	5,771,076
Cemeteries and Burial Grounds ...	2,718,133
Tramways	1,466,610
Harbours, Piers, Docks, and Quays ...	32,777,992
Electric Lighting and Supply ...	1,378,818
Total	£105,015,062

These amounts, it is necessary to observe, do not represent the
present values of the water works, and gas works, &c., nor yet
the original cost, but are merely the balances remaining open
under the various heads. In other words, this is simply an
analysis and apportionment of the undischarged debt, and does
not purport to be the credit side of a balance sheet. A
complete statement of the liabilities and assets of all the local
authorities would be of inestimable value, if it were possible to
procure it. There exists no such thing, however, and from the
nature of the case, it does not seem feasible to draw one up.
Some of the corporations have, it is true, published a valuation
of their possessions, for the information of those who are able
to put faith in such estimates; but the great mass of the local
bodies make no attempt to issue a balance sheet, and confine
their book-keeping to accounts of income and expenditure. So
far, however, as these profit-earning assets are concerned, it is
quite certain that their actual value enormously exceeds the
proportion of the debt by which they are here represented, and
some writers have even affirmed that, if such a thing can be

imagined as the demunicipalization of the municipal trading undertakings, they would be valued for sale to companies at prices fully equal, in the aggregate, to the entire outstanding total of local indebtedness for all purposes. The first and most unexceptionable items in the table are the debts that have been incurred, with general approval, for the purchase or construction of water works and gas works. That water should be cheap, pure, and plentiful is, for sanitary reasons, of the utmost importance; and those local authorities who have taken the supply into their own hands, instead of leaving the consumer at the mercy of a commercial company, have acted with true wisdom. Gas, also, being almost a necessity, as well as an article in the supply of which competition is inadmissible, may legitimately be included in the scope of municipal socialism. The mode of acquiring such undertakings may be described as an application of the joint stock principle. The townspeople go into partnership, so to say, and the town council, as it has no power to issue shares, provides the necessary capital by borrowing. If the management is honest and efficient, there is no reason whatever why debt so incurred should entail any present or prospective expense on the ratepayer, and, as a matter of fact, most of the corporations can afford, after providing for interest, sinking fund, and working expenses, to apply a substantial sum out of the annual revenue in relief of the general rates. To the consumer, the only difference the transfer makes is that his water or gas bill is payable to the town council instead of to a company. Whether corporations have the right to make profit out of their gas and water supply, without specific powers to do so, is a question that has never been tested, but which is considered doubtful. On economic grounds such profits are open to attack, because, firstly, the consumer is taxed, not according to his means, but according to the extent of his consumption; and secondly, because they constitute a tax on production, in the cost of which gas and water are usually important elements. It may be added that the profit derived from water is much less than that from gas, and that, in many instances, the accounts even show a loss, the service charge having been cut down below cost. As regards the remaining items, markets, cemeteries, and tramways are all concerns that are self-supporting, or that can be made so under proper management; while as to harbours and docks, &c., the majority of the loans are not charged on the rates at all. Of capital expenditure that brings in no revenue, we have in the first place the building debt, consisting of:

Schools	£22,970,555
Poor Law purposes (Workhouses, Infirmaries, &c.)	7,773,504
Public Buildings, Offices, &c.	4,958,954
Lunatic Asylums	4,262,968
Police Stations, Gaols, &c.	1,254,469
Baths and Wash-houses	1,469,628
Hospitals	1,141,654
Fire Brigade Stations	693,736
Libraries and Museums	771,138
Slaughter Houses	154,445

Total £45,451,051

This class of outlay cannot, of course, be called productive; but if the necessity or the utility of the objects for which these various descriptions of buildings have been erected is once admitted—and it would be difficult to take exception to any one of them—it is impossible to blame the local authorities for having become their own landlords by capitalizing what they would otherwise have had to pay as rent. Then many millions have been spent on other unproductive purposes, such as these:

Highways, Street Improvements, and Turnpike Roads	£30,143,979
Sewerage and Sewage Disposal Works	23,734,738
Bridges and Ferries	4,351,500
Parks, Pleasure Grounds, Commons, and Open Spaces	5,051,092
Artizans' and Labourers' Dwellings Improvements	4,351,532
Land Drainage and Embankment, River Conservancy, and Sea Defences ...	3,014,270

Total £70,647,111

It is hardly correct, perhaps, to say that the whole of this outlay yields no return. In the case of street improvements, for instance, there is usually the direct advantage of surplus

G

lands, which can be either let or sold, and the indirect
advantage of an increase in the rateable value of the
property benefited. For the use of bridges and ferries, too,
tolls are sometimes charged, and artizans' dwellings are
certainly not let rent free. But, with these trifling
exceptions, the whole of the expenditure is, in a pecuniary
sense, unremunerative, and is represented by assets, most
of which are unrealizable and possess no money value.
Nevertheless, it cannot be stigmatized as waste. To spend
great sums on great objects is often the truest and best
economy. The construction of sewers and drains, the
widening of streets, the clearance of slums, may be works
that produce no income, yet their results, in prolonging human
life and in rendering it better worth living, entitle them to
our most generous appreciation, and the public gain in health
and happiness is, let us hope, an ample set-off against the
pressure of the additional rates. At the same time, we must
not forget that however beneficial such improvements may be,
they are based upon debt, and that borrowing with too great
rapidity and on too large a scale can never be judicious,
whatever the object be. Sanitary science, too, is progressive.
What is held to be right to-day may be proved to be wrong
to-morrow. Millions have been spent in collecting the filth
of towns, and pouring it into our beautiful rivers, to defile
and poison them; millions more may some day have to be
spent in getting it out again. On every side, in fact, there
are indications that money will have to be borrowed in the
future to undo work for the doing of which money is still
owing that was borrowed in the past. Hence, expenditure of
this class cannot be undertaken too carefully; but there is
reason to fear that local authorities have not always gone
very cautiously to work in the past, and that they have been
apt to embark on ambitious, though well-meant, schemes of
improvement without fully counting the cost. If it be asked
what the prospects are as to the future growth and eventual
proportions of the debt, I think the answer must be that the
productive portion seems likely to exhibit a large further
increase, but that the unproductive part, from which we have
most to fear, has almost attained its maximum. Without
borrowing, the local authorities could not have accomplished
a tithe of what they have already done for the community; and
without still further borrowing they will be unable to discharge

the new duties which come with growth of population and with fuller knowledge of the laws of health. But, in most large towns, the heaviest works of this nature—the great main sewers and the network of subsidiary drains—have now been completed, and the amount annually repaid under the operation of the sinking funds ought soon to become greater than the fresh debt. The same is true of the outlay on education: the capital expenditure was greatest in the earlier years, and is now fast diminishing. The productive debt will, as I said, probably go on increasing. There appears every reason to believe that municipalities will not rest satisfied until they have given effect to the principle that no person or persons, except the corporation, shall have any right to interfere with public thoroughfares. Carried to its logical conclusion, this theory implies that all undertakings which meddle with, or claim a partial monopoly of, the streets—such as tramway companies, and all those for the supply of gas, water, hydraulic power, electric light, &c.—will eventually come to be taken over by the local authorities. The aspiration is, perhaps, a laudable one; but its realization, if ever it should come to pass, will mean the addition to local indebtedness of untold millions.

The parent of the prolific family of Corporation Stocks, and the only one of sufficient importance to call for special notice, is the well-known Metropolitan Consolidated Stock, created nearly thirty years ago by the late Board of Works. The Metropolitan Board of Works was originally called into existence by Parliament to cope with the pressing problem of London's drainage, as well as for the prosecution of such other undertakings as the changing circumstances of the metropolis might render necessary. In order to provide a sufficient revenue for this purpose, power was given to levy a rate on the whole of the rateable property within the metropolitan area, as defined by the Metropolis Local Management Act of 1855, but, as might have been expected, it was soon discovered, after getting to work, that heavy capital expenditure could not possibly be met out of current income, and that recourse would have to be had to borrowing. Under these circumstances it was natural, seeing that all the operations of the Board were carried on in obedience to the mandate of Parliament, that the Government should feel itself called upon to assist; and this it was decided to do by lending the credit of the State, to which end the Treasury was authorized to guarantee the repayment of any loans that the Board might find it necessary to contract. Aided by this guarantee, no difficulty was for some years experienced in raising all that was wanted at reasonable rates; but, owing to the fact that the security offered was a bond of entirely unmarketable character, the only lenders, practically speaking, were the Bank of England and the National Debt Commissioners, and, as time passed, it became clear that, sooner or later, other arrangements would have to be made, as these two bodies could not go on lending indefinitely. After a while, too, the Government grew anxious to get rid of its guarantee, as it now perceived that in extending the credit of the State to the metropolis, it had set a bad example to other towns in the kingdom, who might also be soon asking it to act as godfather to their debts. There was no great risk connected with the guarantee, but it formed a bad precedent. By 1869, the Board had run up a debt of eight millions, and, having undertaken works which would require an expenditure of two millions more, it was felt that the time had come to place its finances on a more permanent footing, in order that it might obtain funds with a facility commensurate with the security at its disposal. Accordingly, a Bill was brought in providing for the conversion, with the consent of holders, of all the existing loans into one uniform consolidated stock, the leading feature of which was that it would possess almost every attribute of the public funds, except that, instead of being charged on the Consolidated Fund of the nation, it would be charged on the Consolidated Fund of the metropolis. It also provided that all future loans should be raised in the same way. No actual guarantee was given, but, as the borrowing powers of the Board were placed under the stringent supervision of the Treasury, without whose express sanction no fresh loan could be raised, it might be held that there existed a moral guarantee. The stock was not to be perpetual; in the interests of the future ratepayer it was deemed expedient that the capital should ultimately be extinguished, and it was therefore directed that a sufficient annual instalment should be set aside to redeem all the stock in sixty years from the date of its creation, such sinking fund to be likewise under the control of the Treasury. At the suggestion of the Board, the Bill, as originally presented, gave authority to trustees to invest in the stock, unless expressly prohibited from doing so, but Parliament thought it better to first see how the new security would be received, and therefore struck the clause out. Two years afterwards, however—Metropolitans being then an established success— the clause was re-introduced in a supplementary measure, and was duly passed. To strengthen the parallel with Consols, an Act of 1870 enabled the Board to compound for the stamp duty on transfers, so that since that date the stock has changed hands free of charge. The security consisted of a first charge on all the property possessed by the Board, and on the whole of its revenue from every source. This increases as fast as buildings increase; and as the metropolis of a nation must stand or fall with the nation, its credit is practically the same, provided, of course, that the ratio of metropolitan debt to rateable value is not greater than that of the national debt to the national resources. In any case, it should rank higher than that of any provincial city, though, on the other hand, it must be borne in mind that the metropolitan debt has all been contracted for unremunerative undertakings, while the loans raised by provincial corporations have been partly, and in some instances largely, for productive purposes. The first ten issues of the stock, extending in date from 1869 to 1880, were made identical in their conditions, all bearing interest at 3½ per-cent, and being redeemable in 1929, that is to say, in sixty years from the date of the first issue. It would have been quite feasible to bestow the full term of sixty years on each instalment, but this plan was attended by the drawback that it would have split up the stock into numerous divisions, all of different maturities and of comparatively small amounts, and would thus have injured its marketability, as the balance of advantage between a stock having, say only fifty-two years to run, but forming part of a large issue, and a stock having the full sixty years to run, but of no great amount, would almost invariably be in favour of the former. If carried too far, however, this shortening of the term becomes an injustice, because it burdens the ratepayer with a heavier sinking fund than is necessary; and in 1881, when the Three-and-a-half per-cent Stock had attained the respectable total of £17,000,000, the Board thought it time to make a new departure, both because their improved credit justified a lower rate of interest, and because any fresh addition made to the 1929 stock would have had to be paid off in forty-nine years. Tenders were therefore invited for a Three per-cent Stock, redeemable in 1941, of which the minimum price was fixed at ninety per-cent, and this description of Metropolitan Consols continued to be issued until the Board of Works was superseded by the London County Council. I may here mention, as a fact which is perhaps not generally known, that in 1877, the year in which Treasury Bills were first issued, the Board obtained leave to contract unfunded debt to a limited amount by raising the money needed for temporary purposes on short dated paper, somewhat in the form of the the new floating debt obligations, and repayable like them in not more than twelve months after date, and that the power conferred by the Act of 1877 has been renewed by each successive Annual Money Act, both of the Board and their successors, being kept alive in case it might some day prove useful. The considerations by which the Board of Works were influenced in deciding to lower the rate of interest on their stock in 1881, were equally applicable when their successors, the London County Council, brought out their first issue of £1,000,000 in 1889, and led to a repetition of the former proceeding. Since the introduction of the 3 per-cent stock, of which £10,850,000 had been placed on the market, the improvement in the Board's credit had steadily continued, as shown by the enhanced prices fixed for the successive issues, namely—

1881	90	per-cent minimum.	
1882	96	,,	,,
1883	95½	,,	,,
1884	97½	,,	,,
1885	96½	,,	,,
1886	98	,,	,,
1887	98½	,,	,,

and throughout 1889 the quotation had stood over par. Regard being had to the fact that the Council anticipated many and large future additions to their indebtedness, it was deemed advisable, notwithstanding the obvious disadvantage of having to bring before the public a third description of obligation, to adopt at the outset a form of stock to which it was thought certain, humanly speaking, that the Council would be able to permanently adhere, and a first issue of Two-and-a-half per-cents was therefore announced at the minimum price of 88. In further justification of the course taken by the Council, it was pointed out that the majority of steady investors, and especially trustees, to whom Metropolitan Stock presents great attractions, greatly prefer an investment which is redeemable at a profit, and of which the value must necessarily appreciate, to one that will eventually be paid off below cost, even though the latter be actuarially cheaper, and that they would therefore be more inclined to take a Two-and-a-half per-cent Stock at a discount, than a Three per-cent Stock at a premium. The new Two-and-a-half per-cents—or "Rosebery's" as they were dubbed—now amount to £7,700,000, and have been even a greater success than the Three per-cents. In 1892 the minimum was only 85½; in 1893 it rose to 89; in 1894 to 93½; in 1895 to 101; and in 1896 to 104. The date of redemption is 1949; but the County Council reserve the right to pay them off at par at any time after the 19 March 1920, provided that one year's notice of such repayment shall have been previously given. One feature that distinguishes the debt of the County Council from that of provincial corporations is the fact that a very large proportion of it represents money lent to other bodies. Powers have been given by statute to the London School Board, to the Managers of the Metropolitan Asylums District, and to vestries, district boards, guardians, and other public and local authorities, to borrow from it, and of the total debt of £35,000,000 upwards of one-third has been advanced to outside bodies. You will find on reference to the Official List that the entire stock only shows a diminution from its original amount of £71,686, and it may strike you as strange that the operation of the sinking fund should not bring about a steady-going reduction, such as we are accustomed to in the case of the funds. The reason is that the Council are permitted, instead of buying up their own stock with the annual surplus of income, either to invest it in advances to other bodies, or to employ it in capital expenditure for duly authorized purposes. It is expressly provided, however, that the repayment from such loans shall be hypothecated to the redemption of their own debt, and that no such money shall be so used, unless provision shall be made, in such a manner as the Treasury approve, for repaying the same to the Consolidated Loans Fund at, or before, the date at which Consolidated Stock, redeemable by means of such money, is required to be redeemed at par. In other words, if the funds applicable to the redemption of, say, the 1929 stock are lent out, instead of being used in cancelling the stock, it is essential that the loans should be made repayable before 1929, so that the money may be at hand when wanted. If power to invest the sinking fund in this manner had not been given, the Council would be a heavy loser, as it would have had to buy up its own stock at a heavy premium. Mention has more than once been made of the wide-reaching and constant supervision exercised by the Treasury over the financial arrangements in connection with the Metropolitan Stock. No provincial corporation is under control to anything like the same extent. In fact, beyond having to submit an annual statement of their loans' fund to the Local Government Board, whose suggestions they are expected to treat with due deference, they are left to their own devices. But, in the case of loans raised by the County Council, the fund constituted for paying the dividends and redeeming the principal is under strict supervision, and the Treasury controls the sum which must annually be raised by means of the consolidated rate for the service of the debt.

There still remain one or two minor questions to be noticed in connection with Corporation Stocks. The first is that of redemption. Most of the stocks are described as "Redeemable", and either the date of redemption is tacked on, or the period during which the right to redeem may be exercised. In no instance, it should be noted, is there a premium payable on redemption; the rate is always par. But there are also some stocks marked "Irredeemable," and this designation might lead you to infer that certain of the corporations have been absolved from the duty of repaying, and have been allowed to contract a perpetual debt. All it means is, however, that the stock-holder cannot be paid off against his will; and that, as neither time nor price is fixed for the redemption, the stock can only be cancelled by buying it up in the market at the price of the day. Whether redeemable or not, the borrower must set up a sinking fund, the accumulation of which shall be sufficient to extinguish the stock in a given number of years, as determined by the act authorizing the issue; and the advantage of making it redeemable at a specified time and price is that he knows precisely how much money must be set aside each year in order to meet the obligation at maturity. On the other hand, if the stock be irredeemable, it is not the nominal amount that he must provide for, but the market value, which may be a very different thing. To the citizens of Manchester, for instance, it must be most gratifying to know that their promise to pay £4 per annum is thought so highly of in the market as to be now valued at fifty per-cent premium; but it cannot be equally agreeable to reflect that, owing to their Consolidated Stock not having been made redeemable at par, provision must be made out of the corporate revenues to pay back five-and-a-half millions sterling instead of the three and three-quarter millions, which they borrowed. The objection, therefore, to an irredeemable stock is that every rise in price, after par has once been passed, means a re-adjustment of the sinking fund, and that the borrower is made to suffer for the improvement in his own credit; and this objection has so much force, that power to issue stock of this description is now no longer given by Parliament. Its issue in former years was justified by the supposition that it commanded a better price, but it may be doubted whether any investor would ever distinguish between a stock redeemable at par in fifty or sixty years, and one not subject to redemption at all. Another line of demarcation between corporation stocks is that which separates them into stocks liable to stamp duty and those which are free of the impost. This distinction is of more importance than it looks. The price of a stock depends, to a great extent, on its negotiability, that is to say, on the facility with which the would-be seller can find a would-be buyer, and negotiability is undoubtedly hampered if a tax must be paid every time the stock changes hands. In fact, other things being equal, a stock which is subject to the restriction of transfer-duty will always be at a disadvantage as compared with one that escapes the imposition. The fact that taxation seriously detracts from facility of dealing, and hence from market value, impressed itself strongly upon the Metropolitan Board of Works, very soon after the original issue of their Consolidated Stock, and in 1870, the following year, they obtained powers by a special Act of Parliament to compound for transfer-duty by a single payment of 7s. 6d. per-cent (afterwards raised in 1880 to 12s. 6d. per-cent) on the whole amount of the stock, which at once benefited by the concession. In 1875, as you will remember, the Government brought in a Local Loans Bill, and the provincial corporations, having quite expected that whenever such a measure was introduced they would be offered the same option, experienced some disappointment on finding that such was not the case. "The Metropolitan Board of Works", said Mr. Chamberlain, in opposing the Bill, "has been allowed " to compound for stamp-duty; and until Parliament chooses " to give to provincial corporations the same facilities, it need " not expect that they will take advantage of the Local Loans " Bill." The privilege was extended to them, however, in 1880, and in the Stamp Act of 1891, which is now in force, it is enacted that any county council or corporation may enter into an agreement with the Commissioners of Inland Revenue, if the Commissioners in their discretion think proper, for the composition of the stamp duties chargeable on transfers of their stocks on payment, half-yearly, of 6d. per-cent on the nominal amount. Advantage has been taken of this per-mission to a great extent, and in the prospectus of almost every new issue you now see it stated that transfers will be effected free of stamp duty or other charges, to be followed a week or two afterwards by a short paragraph in the "money article" to the effect that the Commissioners of Inland Revenue have entered into an agreement with the corporation of so-and-so for the composition of the stamp duties payable on transfers of their stock in accordance with the provisions contained in section 115 of "The Stamp Act, 1891."

In addition to the question of liability or non-liability to stamp duty, there are certain other matters of detail associated with the transfer of corporation stocks which call for remark, but which will be found lacking in interest unless we clearly comprehend the principle involved in such arrangements, and the requirements that they ought to fulfil. When a corporation borrows money in order to meet expenditure, of which it is presumably right and proper that the repayment should be spread over a term of years, it would obviously expose itself to extreme inconvenience if the lenders had the right to call in their loans at short notice, and were to exercise such right at a time when the conditions of the money market were not favourable to fresh borrowing. To avoid this risk the loans are made redeemable at fixed dates, and the lender has no power to claim his money until the expiration of the agreed term, which may be anything from thirty years up to sixty or more. But, if that were the whole extent of the bargain, it is more than likely that capitalists would decline to lend on such conditions, or, at any rate, that only very few would be found willing to place their capital beyond control for so long a period, and it is therefore essential that the lender shall be at full liberty, whenever he wishes to realize, to assign his claim to someone else who is willing to buy it of him. The borrower, moreover, must not only undertake to recognize, and act upon the assignment, but is expected to facilitate it as far as he reasonably can by adopting the most workable arrangement. In fact, the easier, the quicker, and the cheaper the claim can be transferred, the easier, the quicker, and the cheaper will the corporation find it possible to borrow. Now, if our cities were in the habit, as foreign municipalities are, of raising loans on bonds to bearer, the title to which passes by delivery, all troublesome transfer formalities would be avoided; but as investors of the class they appeal to mostly prefer (or, if trustees, are even restricted to) a specialized, and therefore safer form of security, they find it advisable to meet the requirements of the market by issuing what we know as stock. This is of the nature of a book debt, the name of the lender, or stock-holder, and the nominal amount of his loan, or stock, being registered by the corporation in a book, just in the same way that a merchant posts in his ledger the names of his creditors, and the sums for which he is indebted to them. In view of the importance of this record, which constitutes the evidence of the stock-holder's title, the duty of keeping a proper register (by register is meant, of course, the whole set of books necessary in connection with the stock), and of inserting therein the names and holdings of all proprietors, is enforced by law, and forms part of every act in which power to create stock is conferred. There are two ways in which stock may be transferred—either by book or by deed. If transferable by signing an entry made in the register itself, the stock is usually designated "Inscribed;" if transferable by signing a separate document or deed of transfer, it is usually described as "Registered." The distinction is quite an artificial one, as "inscribed" and "registered" mean the same thing. Consols are the type of an inscribed stock, and the manner in which they shall be transferred is set forth in section 22 of "The National Debt Act, 1870." "In the offices "of the respective Accountants-General of the Banks of "England and Ireland, books shall continue to be kept wherein "all transfers of stock shall be entered. Every such entry

" shall be conceived in proper words for the purpose of " transfer, and shall be signed by the party making the " transfer, or, if he is absent, by his attorney thereunto " lawfully authorized by writing under his hand and seal, " attested by two or more credible witnesses. The person " to whom a transfer is so made may, if he thinks fit, " underwrite his acceptance thereof. Except as otherwise " provided by Act of Parliament, no other mode of transferring " stock shall be good in law." It is also enacted in section 24 that the banks, before allowing any transfer of stock, " may if " the circumstances of the case appear to them to make it " expedient, require evidence of the title of any person claiming " a right to make the transfer." In " The Colonial Stock Act, 1877 ", which provides for the inscription of stocks issued by the Colonies, and which appears to have been the chief means of bringing inscribed stocks into fashion, we find similar regulations in Section 4: " Colonial Stock to which this Act " applies, while inscribed in a register kept in the United " Kingdom, shall be transferred as follows: (1) The transfer " shall be made only in the register, and shall be signed by the " transferor, or, if he is absent, by his attorney thereunto " lawfully authorized by some writing executed under his hand " and seal and attested. (2) The transferee may, if he thinks " fit, underwrite his acceptance of the transfer." Stock transferable by book is the safest form of security that ingenuity and experience have found it possible to devise. There is as much difference, in fact, between bonds to bearer and inscribed stock, in point of safety, as between a bank note and a crossed " not negotiable " cheque to order. The investor who holds bearer bonds or " scrip stocks " as they are commonly called, besides being exposed to the trouble of detaching and collecting the coupons, must also put up with the anxiety and expense attendant on their safe custody; but in the case of inscribed stock, in addition to the convenience of having the dividend sent to him by post, or paid direct to his banker, it appears absolutely impossible to deprive him of his property without his knowledge. A would-be forger must, in the first place, attend at the office of the registrar and sign the register in the presence of an official, under which circumstances it would require astonishing skill to counterfeit the shareholder's signature sufficiently well to pass muster; and, secondly, he must be accompanied by a respectable stockbroker, or by some one else well known to the registrar, who can answer for his identity. Whether these safeguards are ever overcome is only known to the registrars themselves, but I think I am right in saying that loss by forgery, if it does occur, is never allowed to prejudice the stock-holder. Though the buyer of inscribed stock is not required to attend at the office of the registrar when the transfer into his name is effected, he is at liberty to do so and to sign the register if he thinks fit; and it is certainly advisable that he should be present, in order that a specimen of his signature may at once be on record for comparison. Failing his attendance, the registrar has no apparent means of knowing his signature until it comes in on a dividend warrant. Another precaution by which the safety of inscribed stock is increased is that of giving no certificate. There can be little doubt that the issue of a document containing all particulars of the proprietor's holding must tend to facilitate fraud, if fraud is intended. The distinctive characteristic of inscribed stock is, as I said, the transfer by signature in the register itself, and, as this necessitates the personal attendance of the transferor, or his legally appointed attorney, it would obviously be a great bar to negotiability if the register were kept in an out-of-the-way place. You will, therefore, find that in almost every instance, where stock is transferable in the books, the corporation issuing it has appointed a London banker to act as its agent, and to keep the register on its behalf. It should also be noticed that, practically, the whole of the stocks so domiciled are transferable free of charge and in any amount. This latter proviso is of special convenience to trustees, who, when effecting a change of investment, like to re-invest the exact sum in hand without having a fraction left over. As between inscribed and registered stocks, the great advantage of the former is the rapidity with which a transfer can be effected. The seller's broker, having found a buyer, sends to the bank the particulars necessary for preparing the transfer entry, and, an hour or so afterwards, calls in with his client, who signs the book and also a receipt for the purchase money. This receipt, which is on a form supplied by the bank, is witnessed by the bank clerk, and, on handing it over to the buyer in proof of the transfer having been duly made, payment is effected and the transaction is complete. Compare this procedure with the formalities that must be gone through on transferring property in houses or land, and the perfection to which it has been brought will be better appreciated. Registered stock differs from inscribed stock in the two particulars already indicated, namely, that it is transferable by deed, without attendance, and that a certificate under the seal of the corporation and signed by its authorized official is issued to each stock-holder certifying that he is the registered proprietor of a stated amount of stock. This certificate is not in itself proof of ownership, and the object of granting it is simply to enable the holder to deal more easily with his stock. The only conclusive evidence of title is the entry in the register, the certificate being merely a solemn affirmation under seal that the person named therein actually is on the register as owner of stock to the amount specified. When selling registered stock, a transfer deed is prepared, which must be signed and sealed by both seller and buyer—by the former in token that he transfers, and by the latter in witness that he accepts the transfer. "Sealing" the transfer, which consists in sticking a red paper wafer on a certain spot, is a formality which, nowadays, appears meaningless, but which can be insisted upon. By Stock Exchange custom, the seller—that is to say, the seller's broker—has to make the transfer, and the buyer has to pay the the charges (stamp duty and registration fee, if any). Considerable perplexity, not to say suspicion, is sometimes aroused in the mind of the inexperienced investor, on discovering, when signing a transfer for the sale of stock, that the consideration money named therein does not agree with the sum specified in the contract rendered to him by his broker. If he enquires the reason of the difference, he is referred to a note, which is usually printed at the foot of the deed, and which explains, not so clearly as it might, that "the " consideration money set forth in a transfer may differ from " that which the first seller will receive, owing to sub-sales by " the original buyer; the Stamp Act requires that in such " cases the consideration money paid by the sub-purchaser, " shall be the one inserted in the deed, as regulating the " *ad valorem* duty." Notwithstanding the footnote, however, cases occur in which the transferor undoubtedly considers himself aggrieved in having to sign what appears to be an acknowledgment of a arger sum than he actually receives. The difficulty arises from the fact that stock may change hands again and again before settling day. A. B., the original holder, may, for instance, sell to C. D., at say 99¾ ; C. D. may re-sell to E. F., at par, and E. F. to G. H. at 100¼. As it would obviously be a waste of time and money to execute a chain of transfers, a clearing system is adopted, which there is not time to explain, but the effect of which is that C. D. and E. F. are eliminated from the transaction on payment to them of the respective differences, and that A. B. is represented as transferring direct to G. H. Then comes the question of the consideration money; A. B. sold for £99. 15s., G. H. bought for £100. 5s.; if we insert £99. 15s., the deed must bear a 10s. stamp, if £100. 5s., a 12s. 6d. stamp. To save disputes, the Stamp Act settles the point by deciding that duty must be levied on the amount paid by the transferee. The transfer, therefore, reads: "I, A. B., in consideration of the sum of " one hundred pounds and five shillings, paid by G. H., herein- " after called the said transferee, do hereby bargain, etc.", and A. B. must console himself as best as he can. Registered corporation stocks differ widely in their conditions. Some corporations register transfers free of charge, others exact a fee for doing so; some keep their books open all the year round, others close them for a week or a fortnight at a time to prepare the dividends; some will accept the common form of transfer deed, others require a special form to be used; some will transfer any amount, including shillings and pence, others will only transfer multiples of £10, and so on. The golden rule for the corporations to bear in mind is that the fewer the restrictions the better the stock will be liked, and that, other things being equal, the market is sure, sooner or later, to differentiate in favour of stock which is transferable at all times, in all amounts, and free of all charges.